SIDDHARTHA

HERMANN HESSE

SIDDHARTHA

AN INDIAN POEM

A new translation by Susan Bernofsky

Introduction by Tom Robbins

THE MODERN LIBRARY

NEW YORK

2008 Modern Library Paperback Edition

Introduction copyright © 2006 by Tom Robbins
Translation, translator's preface, glossary, and
biographical note copyright © 2006 by Random House, Inc.
Reading group guide copyright © 2008 by Random House, Inc.

Published in the United States by Modern Library, an imprint of The Random
House Publishing Group, a division of Random House, Inc., New York.

MODERN LIBRARY and the TORCHBEARER Design are registered trademarks of
Random House, Inc.

Originally published in hardcover in the United States by
Modern Library, an imprint of The Random House Publishing
Group, a division of Random House, Inc., in 2006.

LIBRARY OF CONGRESS CATALOGING-IN-PUBLICATION DATA
Hesse, Hermann, 1877–1962.
[Siddhartha, English]
Siddhartha: an Indian poem/Hermann Hesse; a new translation by
Susan Bernofsky; introduction by Tom Robbins.
p. cm.
ISBN 978-0-8129-7478-2
I. Bernofsky, Susan. II. Title

Printed in the United States of America

www.modernlibrary.com

16 18 20 22 24 23 21 19 17

HERMANN HESSE

Hermann Hesse, the Nobel Prize–winning novelist, poet, and critic who enjoyed a cultlike readership among young people during the 1960s, was born in the quiet Black Forest town of Calw, Germany, on July 2, 1877. He was the son and grandson of Protestant clergymen who had served as missionaries in India. Hesse attended the parochial mission school where his father taught and later the Latin school in Göppingen. Having vowed "to be a poet or nothing at all," the headstrong youth fled the seminary in Maulbronn at the age of fourteen. Thereafter Hesse rebelled against all attempts at formal schooling. Instead he pursued a rigorous program of self-study that focused on literature, philosophy, and history and eventually found employment at the Heckenhauer Bookshop in the university town of Tübingen.

In 1899 Hesse published *Romantische Lieder* (*Romantic Songs*), his first book of poetry, and *Eine Stunde hinter Mitternacht* (*An Hour After Midnight*), a series of prose poems hailed by Rainer Maria Rilke as standing "on the periphery of art." Hesse spent the next several years working as a clerk at bookstores in cosmopolitan Basel, where he studied art history and the writings of the Swiss cultural historian Jacob Burckhardt.

Hesse brought out his first novel, *Peter Camenzind,* in 1904. Translated into English in 1969, this story of a failed writer who embarks on a journey to discover the world became the prototype for much of his fiction. Its success enabled him to marry and start a family in the idyllic German village of Gaienhofen. His second novel, *Unterm Rad* (1906; translated as *Beneath the Wheel* in 1968), proved equally popular. The tale of a gifted adolescent crushed by the brutal expectations of his father and teachers, it was proclaimed a "Black Forest *Catcher in the Rye*" by *The National Observer.* Hesse next pondered the sources of creativity in *Gertrud* (1910; translated as *Gertrude* in 1955), a novel of self-appraisal that strongly resembles early works by Thomas Mann. Chronic wanderlust coupled with growing discontent over his bucolic Rousseau-like existence took him on a formative trip to the East Indies in 1911. Hesse's troubled domestic life provided the basis for *Rosshalde* (1914; translated as *Rosshalde* in 1970), the classic tale of a man torn between obligations to his family and the longing for a spiritual fulfillment that exists outside the confines of conventional society. *The Christian Science Monitor* called it "a kind of disguised biography, an account of Hesse's quite private turmoil on the eve of war."

The outbreak of World War I brought a sharp change in Hesse's fortunes. An outspoken pacifist, he volunteered for service at the German consulate in Bern and devoted himself to relief work for German internees and prisoners of war. "The protest against the war, against the raw, bloodthirsty stupidity of mankind, the protest against the 'intellectuals,' especially those who preached war, constituted for me a bitter necessity and duty," Hesse later observed. Yet a series of articles on war and politics written at the time alienated the generally conservative and nationalistic public that had bought his books up until then.

During this same period Hesse endured two personal tragedies, the death of his father and the collapse of his marriage. In 1916 he suffered a complete nervous breakdown and entered a sanatorium near Lucerne to undergo psychoanalysis with a disciple of Carl Jung's. Seeking isolation, Hesse settled by himself in Montagnola, a remote mountain village on the outskirts of Lugano in southeastern Switzerland, in the spring of 1919.

The publication of *Demian* that same year (it appeared in English in 1923) brought Hesse immediate acclaim throughout Europe. Based on his experience with Jungian analysis, this breakthrough novel launched a series of works chronicling the *Weg nach Innen* (inward journey) that he hoped would lead to self-knowledge. In the existential tradition of Nietzsche and Dostoevsky, Hesse portrays the turmoil of a docile young man who is forced to question traditional bourgeois beliefs regarding family, society, and faith. "The electrifying influence exercised on a whole generation just after the First World War by *Demian*...is unforgettable," recalled Thomas Mann. "With uncanny accuracy this poetic work struck the nerve of the times and called forth grateful rapture from a whole youthful generation who believed that an interpreter of their innermost life had risen from their own midst." "The autobiographical undercurrent gives *Demian* an Existentialist intensity and a depth of understanding rare in contemporary fiction," said the *Saturday Review*. "Hesse is not a traditional teller of tales but a novelist of ideas and a moralist of a high order."

"Almost all the prose works I have written are biographies of the soul," Hesse asserted, "monologues in which a single individual is observed in relation to the world and to his own ego." Exploring the oriental religious concepts that became central to his work, he wrote *Siddhartha* (1922; translated into English in 1951), which recounts the spiritual evolution of a man living in India at the time of Buddha. Perhaps more than any other of his novels, *Siddhartha* reflects Hesse's belief that "the true profession of man is to find his way himself." "For me, *Siddhartha* is a more potent medicine than the New Testament," said Henry Miller; Kurt Vonnegut, Jr., deemed it Hesse's "simplest, clearest, most innocent tale of seeking and finding."

Hesse again utilized the tools of psychoanalysis in *Der Steppenwolf* (1927; translated as *Steppenwolf* in 1929), a novel that probes the "two souls" of a reclusive intellectual whose animalistic urges strive for release. Inspired by the dissolute aftermath of Hesse's failed second marriage to a much younger woman, it is arguably his most autobiographical book, one hailed by *The New York Times* as "a savage indictment of bourgeois society." Hesse pursued similar themes in *Narziss und Goldmund* (1930; translated as *Narcissus and Goldmund* in 1968) by presenting parallel biographies of an ascetic monk and a rapturous man of the world. Thomas Mann called *Narcissus and Goldmund* "a poetic novel unique in its purity and fascination." *The New York Times Book Review* agreed. "What makes this short book so limitlessly vast is the body-and-soul-shaking debate that runs through it, which it has the honesty and courage not to resolve: between the flesh and the spirit, art and scientific or religious speculation, action and contemplation, between the wayfaring and the sedentary in us."

In 1931, Hesse married for a third time and moved to a new home in Montagnola. His happiness is reflected in *Die Morgenlandfahrt* (1932; translated as *The Journey to the East* in 1957), a personal fairy tale in which he reaffirms his belief in the superiority of the realms of art and thought. With Hitler's rise to power, Hesse (by then a Swiss citizen) began harboring Jewish refugees and blacklisted artists fleeing the Third Reich. Soon his work was declared "undesirable" in Nazi Germany. In 1932 he started writing the futuristic novel that endures as his magnum opus. Published in 1943, *Das Glasperlenspiel* (translated as *The Glass Bead Game* in 1969) takes place in the year 2400 in a utopian land where artists and intellectuals strive to attain "perfection, pure being, the fullness of reality." "The sublime work of [Hesse's] old age, *The Glass Bead Game* [is] drawn from all sources of human culture, both East and West," observed Thomas Mann. "This chaste and daring work, full of fantasy and at the same time highly intellectual, is full of tradition, loyalty, memory, secrecy—without being in the least derivative." Admired as well by T. S. Eliot and André Gide, it is widely seen as the key to a full understanding of Hesse's thought.

Hesse was awarded the Nobel Prize for Literature in 1946. *Krieg und Frieden*, his lifelong reflections on war and politics, came out the same year; in 1971 it appeared in English as *If the War Goes On*. One of Europe's grand old men of letters, Hesse spent his final years in seclusion at Montagnola compiling volumes of his poetry, essays, and correspondence. Unaware that he was suffering from leukemia, Hermann Hesse died in his sleep from a cerebral hemorrhage on August 9, 1962. "The entire work of Hesse is a poetic effort for emancipation," said André Gide. "In each of [his books] I refind the same indecision of soul; its contours are illusive and its aspirations, infinite." Hesse's longtime friend and countryman Thomas Mann remarked, "For me his lifework, with its roots in native German romanticism, for all its occasional strange individualism, its now humorously petulant and now mystically yearning estrangement from the world and the times, belongs to the highest and purest spiritual aspirations and labors of our epoch."

Hesse's call for self-realization coupled with his celebration of Eastern mysticism earned him a huge following among America's counterculture in the decade after his death. "Rarely, since a generation of young Europeans decked themselves out in the blue frock coat and yellow vest of Goethe's Werther, has the youth culture of an age responded so rapturously to a writer," observed the Hesse scholar Theodore Ziolkowski in 1973. Hesse "is deeply loved by those among the American young who are questing," wrote Kurt Vonnegut, Jr. "The wanderers of Hesse always find something satisfying—holiness, wisdom, hope." And the London *Times Literary Supplement* concluded, "The Hesse we read today is in fact no longer the bittersweet elegist of Wilhelmine Germany, the anguished intellectual *entre deux guerres,* the serene hermit of Montagnola *après* Nobel. The cult has adjusted the kaleidoscope of Hesse's works in such a way as to bring into focus a Hesse for the 1970s: environmentalist, war opponent, enemy of a computerized technocracy, who seeks heightened awareness . . . and who is prepared to sacrifice anything but his integrity for the sake of his freedom."

CONTENTS

SIDDHARTHA

PART ONE

PART TWO

INTRODUCTION

Tom Robbins

Dostoevsky is credited with having invented the psychological novel—although considering the millions of pages of tediously internalized, angst-ridden prose that have fluttered in on the Russian's long, dark coattails (fiction that has been both a crime and a punishment), maybe "accused of" rather than "credited with" is the more appropriate phrase.

The problem, for writers and readers alike, with all this inward gazing is how few of us ever gaze in far enough to justify the strain. To reap lasting rewards, to escape the briar patch of perpetuated trauma, the gazer must delve beneath the ego level, the personality level, the level of genetic predisposition and environmental conditioning, must penetrate more deeply even than the archetypal underworld. One of the very rare Western authors not only to plumb those arcane depths but to do so in a narratively entertaining, stylistically engaging fashion (thereby making Dostoevsky's overheated lemons into cool and refreshing, though highly potent, lemonade), was Hermann Hesse.

Steeped in German mysticism and Asian philosophy (he traveled twice to the Far East), and having expanded his awareness by ingesting on several occasions hallucinogenic mescaline, Hesse (1877–1962) was perhaps ideally qualified to invent a new kind of psychological novel. Gradually he had come to recognize that very often despair, misery, and degeneration are simply the price we're charged for our bad attitudes and myopic vision. Once he became convinced that we humans can alter reality by altering our perceptions of it, the lid was off the pitcher. Hesse went to his writing desk and poured the nectar.

Having shifted his focus from the concerns that had traditionally occupied serious novelists (socio-economic conflicts, physical challenges, romantic entanglements); from familiar territory to regions outside the zone of normal expectations, Hesse was now in a position to compose startling new novels-of-ideas, novels containing such ideas, in fact, as had seldom if ever been expressed in modern literature.

Like the existentialists, Hesse seemed to view the mass of humanity as one big twitchy, squealy, many-headed beast caught in a trap of its own making. Unlike Camus and Sartre, however, he suspected the trap might be sprung through a kind of alchemical transformation and/or spiritual transcendence.

Alchemical transformation he explored brilliantly in his 1927 masterpiece, *Steppenwolf,* destined to become, for obvious reasons, a favorite of the psychedelic counterculture. As far out as it was, however, *Steppenwolf* was pungent with the musk of Old Europe. Five years earlier, exhaling a sandalwood effluvium of borrowed spirituality, he penned a shorter, though no less courageous, novel that follows the corkscrew path of a well-born East Indian who is fervently, if somewhat erratically, searching for ultimate meaning in life: an ambitious "golden child" whose goals do not lie at the top of any ordinary ladder, a restless traveler whose destination could not be found on any map.

In the parlance of cinema, *Siddhartha* would qualify as a "road movie." But because the protagonist's personal motto throughout his various and sometimes contradictory stages of development remains "Thinking, waiting, fasting," and because he wanders barefoot in an age (circa 500 B.C.) when there was nary a pedal to push to the metal, he logs in a tiny fraction of the mileage accumulated by, say, the characters in *On the Road*.

Siddhartha nonetheless does bear a superficial resemblance to Kerouac's novel, in which, despite their relentless pursuit of kicks, the beatniks maintain a fascination with Eastern philosophy, and, however crudely, demonstrate a hunger for spiritual illumination. For his part, Siddhartha also takes a detour through the pleasurelands of flesh and fermentation before moving on to more refined ground.

Judeo-Christian-Islamic ethos to the contrary, there is an extremely blurry line between an appetite for life and a yearning for God, and both Kerouac and Hesse intuited this sensual/spiritual interface, though, each for his own reasons, neither was entirely comfortable with a melting of the largely artificial boundary: Kerouac's fictional hipsters were restrained by the author's own Catholic guilt, whereas Hesse's pilgrim temporarily loses himself in the realm of the senses, thereby derailing his quest for union with the Absolute and illustrating the perils that can arise when the spirit is voted out of office by the body. (It should go without saying that the opposite is equally as dangerous.)

At this point it might be tempting to compare *Siddhartha* to another fine novel about a young man's quest for meaning, W. Somerset Maugham's *The Razor's Edge*, but while parallels definitely exist, the differences between the two books are nearly as pronounced as those between a Chicago hot dog and a Bombay curry. Maugham's searcher, Larry Darrell, is a Midwestern American who starts out not knowing squat about matters of enlightenment. Siddhartha, on the other hand, is up to his shining brow in holy ritual even as a boy. The dissatisfied Darrell, merely "hoping to make something interesting of his life," begins by rejecting a career in bourgeois business. The dissatisfied Siddhartha, a brahmin's son, commences *his* journey by rejecting the same sacred methodologies that Darrell eventually ends up embracing (to his betterment, it must be said).

Indeed, Siddhartha's journey may be plotted as a long succession of jettisoned doctrines and renounced dogmas. Everyone around him believes him destined to mature into an all-star brahmin, the LeBron James of Hindu theology, but unfulfilled by ablutions, scriptures and discourse, he walks away from guaranteed success in the religious arena. Later, he also spurns an opportunity to hang with Gautama (the Sublime One, himself), obviously not knowing—or not caring—which side his bread is buddhaed on.

Siddhartha turns orthodox Hinduism inside out, flicks the translucent lint from Buddha's much-contemplated navel, and deserts the extremist samanas with whom he's been starving himself in the forest; becoming increasingly convinced that "a true seeker could not accept doctrine." Finally, the seeker even rejects seeking, concluding that ultimate reality can never be captured in a net made of thought, and that "knowing has no worse enemy than the desire to know." Strong stuff.

Lest his ongoing rebellion smack of impudence or even nihilism, it can be reported, without giving away too much to the first-time reader, that Siddhartha's litany of "No's" leads him to one loud, resounding "Yes!" He trashes the This, he torches the That, only to arrive at an acceptance of the All. In the end, even mankind's "nervous, proud little ego" is no longer despised as our worst enemy but rather accepted as just another piece of foolishness to be smiled at affectionately and calmly observed.

To reach that plateau of serene affirmation, Siddhartha has to reduce mainstream Hinduism and nascent Buddhism to their essence, and what remains in the bottom of his double boiler is a systemless system that perhaps most closely resembles Zen.

For reasons of historical accuracy, Zen could not have been mentioned in Hesse's book, but the attitudes that were to engender Zen, to shape it, are very much at play here. There is, however, one glaring discrepancy. The Zen perspective is in many ways a comic perspective, and *Siddhartha* is as humorless as a hot rock. (We shouldn't blame this on Hesse's Germanic temperament. Germans actually have a great sense of humor: Otherwise there'd be no such thing as lederhosen.)

Those of us who believe that wisdom unleavened by humor is fundamentally unwise are destined to be confounded by *Siddhartha,* for as arid of cosmic wit as it is, it radiates more genuine wisdom than just about any novel ever published. How can this be? Well, although *Siddhartha* isn't exactly a barrel of laughs, it does pay tribute to laughter. At the saddest moment in his life, the protagonist hears a river laughing at his despair, laughing at time and at all the world, and, buoyed, is moved to ask himself if existence is not a comedy.

Siddhartha is attuned to the river by his friend and confidant, a simple ferryman who is perhaps the true buddha in this tale; and the eternal freedom resonant in the stream's thousand voices emboldens the pilgrim, too, to let go, loosen up, and become eternally free. If the soundtrack of *Steppenwolf* is the music of Mozart, drawing down genius from the stars, *Siddhartha*'s soundtrack is a raga of river burble and leaf rustle: elementary songs with a natural immunity to the virus of opportunism that seems sooner or later to infect society's every attempt at organized expression.

Hardly a repository of proto–New Age, feel-good fluff,

Siddhartha totes some heavy emotional freight—but it bears its load with the attentive grace of a Zen master carrying a bundle of firewood back to his hut.

A tough little wind-tossed blossom of a novel, *Siddhartha* comes to rest in a place of deep wisdom. Ah, but while it has continued, decade after decade, to inspire its readers, to expose them to the mysteries of wisdom, it has never pretended that it could make them more wise. The road to enlightenment is an unpaved road, closed to public transportation. It is because we must travel its last miles unencumbered and alone that Hesse has *his* traveler remind us emphatically that "Wisdom cannot be passed on." And that reminder may be the hardest, most valuable jewel in this literary lotus.

—

TOM ROBBINS is the author of eight offbeat but popular novels, all of which remain in print. They include *Even Cowgirls Get the Blues, Jitterbug Perfume, Fierce Invalids Home from Hot Climates,* and *Villa Incognito.* His new mostly nonfiction collection is *Wild Ducks Flying Backward.*

TRANSLATOR'S PREFACE

Hermann Hesse's *Siddhartha: An Indian Poem* is a novel that inhabits two distinct locations: an imagined India of the fifth and sixth centuries B.C., and a Machine Age Europe in which the heightened efficiency and automation of everyday life prompted a great many writers, not just Hesse, to retreat into various sorts of pastoral idylls. These modern idylls were generally set not in mountains and meadows but in the landscapes of interior existence. Less than a generation had passed since Sigmund Freud had mapped out the contours of the human psyche, and Hesse was one of many writers of the period (among them Robert Musil, Arthur Schnitzler, Frank Wedekind, Hugo von Hofmannsthal, Robert Walser, Thomas Mann, and Franz Kafka) to devote themselves to exploring the mental—and often sexual—coming-of-age of young men in a world that took little interest in their development as individuals. Hesse began writing *Siddhartha* in 1919, only a year after the close of the First World War, which had devastated Europe with unprecedented violence. This war, fought with the modern machinery of airplanes, tanks, and bombs, took the lives of 8.5 million men across Europe (with a further 7.8

million missing in action), and of those who returned home, many were physically and psychologically scarred. There was scarcely a family anywhere in Germany not directly impacted by this war. Before it was over, Hesse fled to neutral Switzerland, where he fought bitterly against the war machine in an impassioned series of newspaper articles while undergoing psychoanalysis with a pupil of Carl Jung's.

Siddhartha, then, with its emphasis on soul-searching and harmony, on stillness, balance, and peace, represented an escape to a world in which a boy could grow up untouched by strife and devote his life to seeking the path of his own personal development. That this quest intersects only loosely with the Buddhist and Hindu doctrines Hesse invokes in his novel need not trouble us as readers: Siddhartha is a child of his time, a fin de siècle youth who has put on a loincloth and monk's robe for a fancy-dress ball. The novel is not intended to show us India as it was in the age of the Buddha. (One might notice, for one thing—as Tom Robbins did when he read this new translation—that Hesse has populated his novel with improbable fauna: chimpanzees and jaguars, creatures to be found in India only in zoos.) In fact, *Siddhartha* is nothing less than a modern bildungsroman in which Indian religions—pursued here not from an ethnographic impulse, out of a desire for accuracy, but rather as dictated by the author's inspiration—become a powerful metaphor whose very distance from the European reality of the time just goes to show how unbearable that reality was.

Hesse subtitled *Siddhartha* "eine indische Dichtung," "an Indian poem." The word *Dichtung* might also have been translated as "fiction," but the overtones of the word are too postmodern. *Dichtung* also has a distinguished history in Germany, a country that calls itself the land of poets and thinkers; it appears, for example, in the title of Johann Wolfgang von Goethe's memoir *Poetry and Truth*, where it signifies not only written lines of verse, but make-believe in general. In truth, Hesse's novel *is* a work of poetry, and I have tried to preserve his attention to language in my translation. *Siddhartha* is suffused with a sense of harmony and measure, and Hesse's sentences tend to fall just so, with a great deal of gravitas and a certain decadent lushness. He often repeats phrases, which has the effect of a chant or incantation. Thus it is crucial for the sentences of the translation to have an elegant, melodious cadence, rich in assonance—this is what Hesse reads like in German. What makes the book luminous in the original is the way the quest for perfection/Nirvana is reflected in the quiet beauty of the prose.

Certain choices I have made in the translation are worth noting. The German word *Ich*—literally "I" in German—corresponds roughly to the English "self," but it is also the word Freud picked for what in English is called the "ego," and so I translate it as one or the other as context demands; for Hesse, the word meant both at once. The German *Lieber*—literally "dear one" or "beloved one"—is such a common form of address and appears so often in the novel that I have given it multiple incarnations as "friend," "my friend," "dear friend," and even, in one instance, "my love." I thought about translating Hesse's *Lehre* as "dharma," since that word is now part of our vocabulary in English, but decided to stick with the English equivalents "doctrine" and "teachings," which serve just as well. Finally, Hesse's novel contains a striking quantity of language commonly associated with Christian theology, and I was careful to preserve these echoes in the translation as well, with words like "bliss," "redemption," "preach," "novice," "saint," and "sermon," as well as Govinda's impassioned question to his friend Siddhartha: "Why have you forsaken me?"

I am grateful to Kristin Scheible and Richard Davis, who generously shared with me their expertise on Indian religions; to the Goethe-Institute Chicago, which sponsored a stay at the Literarisches Colloquium Berlin while I worked on the translation; to Judy Sternlight and Janet Baker for their editorial ministrations; and to my husband, Don Byron, for more than I can say.

—SUSAN BERNOFSKY

PART ONE

Dedicated to Romain Rolland,
my esteemed friend

THE SON OF THE BRAHMIN

In the shade of the house, in the sunlight on the riverbank where the boats were moored, in the shade of the *sal* wood and the shade of the fig tree, Siddhartha grew up, the Brahmin's handsome son, the young falcon, together with his friend Govinda, the son of a Brahmin. Sunlight darkened his fair shoulders on the riverbank as he bathed, performed the holy ablutions, the holy sacrifices. Shade poured into his dark eyes in the mango grove as he played with the other boys, listened to his mother's songs, performed the holy sacrifices, heard the teachings of his learned father and the wise men's counsels. Siddhartha had long since begun to join in the wise men's counsels, to practice with Govinda the art of wrestling with words, to practice with Govinda the art of contemplation, the duty of meditation. He had mastered *Om*, the Word of Words, learned to speak it soundlessly into himself while drawing a breath, to speak it out soundlessly as his breath was released, his soul collected, brow shining with his mind's clear thought. He had learned to feel Atman's presence at the core of his being, inextinguishable, one with the universe.

Joy leaped into his father's heart at the thought of his son, this studious boy with his thirst for knowledge; he envisioned him growing up to be a great wise man and priest, a prince among Brahmins.

Delight leaped into his mother's breast when she beheld him, watched him as he walked and sat and stood, Siddhartha, the strong handsome boy walking on slender legs, greeting her with flawless grace.

Love stirred in the hearts of the young Brahmin girls when Siddhartha walked through the streets of their town with his radiant brow, his regal eye, his narrow hips.

But none of them loved him more dearly than Govinda, his friend, the Brahmin's son. He loved Siddhartha's eyes and his sweet voice, loved the way he walked and the flawless grace of his movements; he loved all that Siddhartha did and all he said and most of all he loved his mind, his noble, passionate thoughts, his ardent will, his noble calling. Govinda knew: This would be no ordinary Brahmin, no indolent pen pusher overseeing the sacrifices, no greedy hawker of incantations, no vain, shallow orator, no wicked, deceitful priest, and no foolish, good sheep among the herd of the multitude. Nor did he, Govinda, have any intention of becoming such a creature, one of the tens of thousands of ordinary Brahmins. His wish was to follow Siddhartha, the beloved, splendid one. And if Siddhartha should ever become a god, if he were ever to take his place among the Radiant Ones, Govinda wished to follow him, as his friend, his companion, his servant, his spear bearer, his shadow.

Thus was Siddhartha beloved by all. He brought them all joy, filled them with delight.

To himself, though, Siddhartha brought no joy, gave no delight. Strolling along the rosy pathways of the fig garden, seated in the blue-tinged shade of the Grove of Contemplation, washing his limbs in the daily expiatory baths, performing sacrifices in the deep-shadowed mango wood, with his gestures of flawless grace, he was beloved by all, a joy to all, yet was his own heart bereft of joy. Dreams assailed him, and troubled thoughts—eddying up from the waves of the river, sparkling down from the stars at night, melting out of the sun's rays; dreams came to him, and a disquiet of the soul wafting in the smoke from the sacrifices, murmuring among the verses of the Rig-Veda, welling up in the teachings of the old Brahmins.

Siddhartha had begun to harbor discontent. He had begun to feel that his father's love and the love of his mother, even the love of his friend Govinda, would not always and forever suffice to gladden him, content him, sate him, fulfill him. He had begun to suspect that his venerable father and his other teachers, all wise Brahmins, had already given him the richest and best part of their wisdom, had already poured their plenty into his waiting vessel, yet the vessel was not full: His mind was not content, his soul not at peace, his heart restless. The ablutions were good, but they were only water; they could not wash away sin, could not quench his mind's thirst or dispel his heart's fear. The sacrifices and the invocations of the gods were most excellent—but was this all? Did the sacrifices bring happiness? And what of the gods? Was it really Prajapati who had created the world? Was it not rather Atman, He, the Singular, the One and Only? Weren't the gods mere shapes, creations like you and me, subject to time, transitory? And was it then good, was it proper, was it meaningful, a noble act, to sacrifice to the gods? To whom else should one sacrifice, to whom else show devotion, if not to Him, the Singular, Atman? And where was Atman to be found, where did He reside, where did His eternal heart lie beating? Where else but within oneself, in the innermost indestructible core each man carries inside him. But where, where was this Self, this innermost, utmost thing? It was not flesh and bone, it was not thought and not consciousness, at least according to the wise men's teachings. Where was it then, where? To penetrate to this point, to reach the Self, oneself, Atman—could there be any other path worth seeking? Yet this was a path no one was showing him; it was a path no one knew, not his father, not the teachers and wise men, not the holy songs intoned at the sacrifices! They knew everything, these Brahmins and their holy books, everything, and they had applied themselves to everything, more than everything: to the creation of the world, the origins of speech, of food, of inhalation and exhalation; to the orders of the senses, the deeds of the gods—they knew infinitely many things—but was there value in knowing all these things without knowing the One, the Only thing, that which was important above all else, that was, indeed, the sole matter of importance?

To be sure, many verses in the holy books, above all the Upanishads of the Sama-Veda, spoke of this innermost, utmost thing: splendid verses. "Your soul is the entire world" was written there, and it was written as well that in sleep, the deepest sleep, man entered the innermost core of his being and dwelt in Atman. There was glorious wisdom in these verses; all the knowledge of the wisest men was collected here in magic words, pure as the honey collected by bees. It was not to be disregarded, this massive sum of knowledge that had been collected here by countless generations of wise Brahmins.

But where were the Brahmins, where the priests, where the wise men or penitents who had succeeded not merely in knowing this knowledge but in living it? Where was the master who had been able to transport his own being-at-home-in-Atman from sleep to the waking realm, to life, to all his comings and goings, his every word and deed?

Siddhartha knew a great many venerable Brahmins, above all his father, a pure, learned, utterly venerable man. Worthy of admiration was his father, still and regal his bearing, his life pure, his words full of wisdom; fine and noble thoughts resided in his brow. But even he, who was possessed of such knowledge, did he dwell in bliss, did he know peace? Was not he too only a seeker, a man tormented by thirst? Was he not compelled to drink again and again from the holy springs, a thirsty man drinking in the sacrifices, the books, the dialogues of the Brahmins? Why must he, who was without blame, wash away sin day after day, labor daily to cleanse himself, each day anew? Was not Atman within him? Did not the ancient source of all springs flow within his own heart? This was what must be found, the fountainhead within one's own being; you had to make it your own! All else was searching, detour, confusion.

Such was the nature of Siddhartha's thoughts; this was his thirst, this his sorrow.

Often he recited to himself the words of a Chandogya Upanishad: "Verily, the name of the Brahman is Satyam; truly, he who knows this enters each day into the heavenly world." It often seemed near at hand, this heavenly world, but never once had he succeeded in reaching it, in quenching that final thirst. And of all the wise and wisest men he knew and whose teachings he enjoyed, not a single one had succeeded in reaching it, this heavenly world; not one had fully quenched that eternal thirst.

"Govinda," Siddhartha said to his friend. "Govinda, beloved one, come under the banyan tree with me; let us practice *samadhi.*"

To the banyan they went and sat down beneath it, Siddhartha here and Govinda at a distance of twenty paces. As he sat down, ready to speak the *Om*, Siddhartha murmured this verse:

> "*Om* is the bow; the arrow is soul.
> Brahman is the arrow's mark;
> Strike it with steady aim."

When the usual time for the meditation exercise had passed, Govinda arose. Evening had come; it was time to begin the ablutions of the eventide. He called Siddhartha's name; Siddhartha gave no answer. Siddhartha sat rapt, his eyes fixed unmoving upon a far distant point; the tip of his tongue stuck out from between his teeth; he seemed not to be breathing. Thus he sat, cloaked in *samadhi,* thinking *Om,* his soul an arrow on its way to Brahman.

One day, Samanas passed through Siddhartha's town: ascetic pilgrims, three gaunt lifeless men, neither old nor young, with bloody, dust-covered shoulders, all but naked, singed by the sun, shrouded in isolation, foreign to the world and hostile to it, strangers and wizened jackals among men. The hot breath of air that followed them bore the scent of silent passion, a duty that meant destruction, the merciless eradication of ego.

In the evening, when the hour of contemplation had passed, Siddhartha said to Govinda, "Tomorrow morning, my friend, Siddhartha will go to the Samanas. He will become a Samana."

Govinda turned pale when he heard these words and saw in his friend's impassive face a resolve as unwavering as an arrow shot from the bow. At once, with a single glance, Govinda realized: Now it is beginning, now Siddhartha is on his way, now his destiny is beginning to bud and, along with it, mine as well. And he turned as pale as a dried-out banana peel.

"Oh, Siddhartha," he cried, "will your father permit this?"

Siddhartha glanced over at him like a man awakening. Swift as an arrow he read Govinda's soul, read the fear, read the devotion.

"Oh, Govinda," he said softly, "let us not squander words. Tomorrow at daybreak I begin the life of a Samana. Speak no more of it."

Siddhartha went into the room where his father was seated upon a mat made of bast fiber; he came up behind him and remained standing there until his father felt there was someone behind him. "Is that you, Siddhartha?" the Brahmin said. "Then say what you have come here to say."

Said Siddhartha, "With your permission, my father. I have come to tell you that it is my wish to leave your house tomorrow and join the ascetics. I must become a Samana. May my father not be opposed to my wish."

The Brahmin was silent and remained silent so long that the stars drifted in the small window and changed their shape before the silence in the room reached its end. Mute and motionless stood the son with his arms crossed, mute and motionless upon his mat sat the father, and the stars moved across the sky. Then the father said, "It is not fitting for a Brahmin to utter sharp, angry words. But my heart is filled with displeasure. I do not wish to hear this request from your lips a second time."

Slowly the Brahmin rose to his feet. Siddhartha stood in silence with his arms crossed.

"Why do you wait here?" the father asked.

"You know why I wait," Siddhartha replied.

Full of displeasure, the father left the room; full of displeasure, he went to his bed and lay down.

An hour later, as no sleep would enter his eyes, the Brahmin got up, paced back and forth, and went out of the house. He looked through the small window of the room and saw Siddhartha standing there, his arms crossed, unmoving. The light cloth of his tunic was shimmering pale. His heart full of disquiet, the father went back to bed.

An hour later, as no sleep would yet enter his eyes, the Brahmin got up once more, paced back and forth, and went out of the house. The moon had risen. He looked through the window into the room; there stood Siddhartha, unmoving, his arms crossed, moonlight gleaming on his bare shins. His heart full of apprehension, the father returned to bed.

An hour later, and again two hours later, he went out and looked through the small window to see Siddhartha standing there: in the moonlight, in the starlight, in the darkness. He went again from hour to hour, in silence, looked into the room, and saw his son standing there unmoving, and his heart filled with anger, with disquiet, with trepidation, with sorrow.

And in the last hour of night before day began, he got up once more, went into the room, and saw the youth standing there; he looked tall to him and like a stranger.

"Siddhartha," he said, "why do you wait here?"

"You know why."

"Will you remain standing here, waiting, until day comes, noon comes, evening comes?"

"I will remain standing here, waiting."

"You will grow tired, Siddhartha."

"I will grow tired."

"You will fall asleep, Siddhartha."

"I will not fall asleep."

"You will die, Siddhartha."

"I will die."

"And you would rather die than obey your father?"

"Siddhartha has always obeyed his father."

"So you will give up your plan?"

"Siddhartha will do as his father instructs him."

The first light of day fell into the room. The Brahmin saw that Siddhartha's knees were trembling quietly. In Siddhartha's face he saw no trembling; his eyes gazed into the distance straight before him. The father realized then that Siddhartha was no longer with him in the place of his birth. His son had already left him behind.

The father touched Siddhartha's shoulder.

"You will go," he said. "Go to the forest and be a Samana. If you find bliss in the forest, come and teach it to me. If you find disappointment, return to me and we will once more sacrifice to the gods side by side. Now go and kiss your mother; tell her where you are going. It is time for me to go to the river and begin my first ablutions."

He took his hand from his son's shoulder and went out. Siddhartha lurched to one side when he tried to walk. Forcing his limbs into submission, he bowed before his father and went to find his mother to do as his father had instructed.

In the first light of dawn, as he was slowly leaving the town on his stiff legs, a shadow rose up beside the last hut, a shadow that had been crouching there and now joined the pilgrim: Govinda.

"You came," said Siddhartha, and smiled.

"I came," Govinda said.

AMONG THE SAMANAS

In the evening of this day they caught up with the ascetics, the gaunt Samanas, and offered to accompany them, promising obedience. They were accepted.

Siddhartha gave his robe to a poor Brahmin on the road. He now wore only his loincloth and an earth-hued wrap that had been cut but not sewn. He ate only once a day, and only food that had not been cooked. He fasted for fifteen days. He fasted for twenty-eight days. The flesh vanished from his thighs and cheeks. Hot tears flickered in his enlarged eyes, the nails grew long on his withering fingers, and from his chin grew a dry, patchy beard. His gaze was like ice when he came upon women; his mouth twitched with contempt when he walked through a town full of elegantly clothed people. He observed merchants doing business, princes on their way to hunt, the bereaved mourning their dead, whores soliciting, doctors tending to patients, priests choosing the day when the seeds would be sown, lovers making love, mothers nursing their infants—and all these things were unworthy of being looked upon by him; it was all a lie, it all stank, stank of lies, it all gave the illusion of meaning and happiness and beauty, and all of it was just putrefaction that no one would admit to. Bitter was the taste of the world. Life was a torment.

Before him, Siddhartha saw a single goal: to become empty, empty of thirst, empty of want, empty of dream, empty of joy and sorrow. To let the ego perish, to be "I" no longer, to find peace with an empty heart and await the miraculous with thoughts free of Self. This was his goal. When all ego had been overcome, had perished, when every longing and every drive in his heart had fallen silent, only then could the Utmost awaken, the great secret, that innermost core of being that is no longer Self.

Silent, Siddhartha stood beneath the sun's vertical rays, glowing with pain, glowing with thirst—stood there until he no longer felt pain or thirst. Silent, he stood in monsoon season; water trickled from his hair onto freezing shoulders, over freezing hips and legs, but the penitent stood until shoulders and legs no longer froze, until they fell silent and were still. Silent, he crouched among thornbushes while blood dripped from his burning skin and pus dripped from open wounds; Siddhartha remained there unyielding, remained motionless until no more blood flowed, nothing pricked any longer, nothing burned.

Siddhartha sat upright and learned to conserve his breath, learned to get by with little air, learned to shut off his breathing. He learned, beginning with his breath, to slow the beating of his heart, learned to decrease his heartbeats until there were few of them, almost none at all.

Instructed by the eldest of the Samanas, Siddhartha practiced the eradication of ego, practiced *samadhi* according to new Samana rules. A heron flew over the bamboo forest—and Siddhartha received the heron into his soul, flew over forests and mountains, was heron, ate fish, felt the pangs of heron hunger, spoke in heron squawks, died a heron death. A dead jackal lay on the sandy bank—and Siddhartha's soul slipped into the corpse, was dead jackal, lay on the beach, grew bloated, stank, decayed, was torn apart by hyenas and flayed by vultures, became a skeleton, became dust, blew into the fields. And Siddhartha's soul returned—it had died, had decayed, become dust, it had tasted the bleak euphoria of the cyclical journey, and then, freshly thirsty, it waited, crouching like a hunter for the gap in the cycle where escape was possible, where the end of causality began, an eternity free of sorrow. He killed off his senses, he killed off his memory, he slipped from his Self to enter a thousand new shapes—was animal, was cadaver, was stone, was wood, was water—and each time he awakened he found himself once more. The sun would be shining, or else the moon, and he was once more a Self oscillating in the cycle; he felt thirst, overcame the thirst, felt new thirst.

Siddhartha learned many things from the Samanas; he learned to walk many paths leading away from the Self. He walked the path of eradication of ego through pain, through the voluntary suffering and overcoming of pain, of hunger, of thirst, of weariness. He walked the path of eradication of ego through meditation, using thought to empty the mind of all its notions. These and other paths he learned to walk. A thousand times he left his Self behind, spent hours and days at a time liberated from it. But just as all these paths led away from the Self, the end of each of them returned him to it. Even if Siddhartha fled the Self a thousand times, lingering in nothingness, in the animal, in stone, his return was unavoidable, the hour inescapable when he found himself once more, in sunlight or moonlight, in shade or rain, and once more he was Self, was Siddhartha, and once more he felt the torments of the cycle imposed on him.

Beside him lived Govinda, his shadow, walking the same paths, subjecting himself to the same exertions. Rarely did they speak of anything beyond what duty and their exercises required. Sometimes they walked together through the villages to beg food for themselves and their teachers.

"What say you, Govinda," Siddhartha inquired on one such excursion, "what say you: Are we now farther than we were? Have we reached goals?"

Govinda replied, "We have learned and we are learning. You will be a great Samana, Siddhartha. You have mastered each exercise swiftly and have often been admired by the elder Samanas. You will be a holy man one day, O Siddhartha."

Said Siddhartha, "This is not how matters appear to me, my friend. Everything I have learned to this day from the Samanas, O Govinda, I might have learned more quickly and simply. In some bar in a street full of whores, my friend, among the cart drivers and dice players, I might have learned these things."

Govinda said, "Siddhartha is joking with me. How could you have learned *samadhi,* the holding of the breath, the insensibility to hunger and pain among such miserable creatures?"

But Siddhartha spoke softly, as if speaking to himself. "What is meditation? What is leaving the body? What is fasting? What is holding the breath? It is all an escape from Self, it is a brief respite from the torment of being Self, a brief numbing of the pain and senselessness of life. This is the same escape, the same numbness the ox driver finds at the inn when he drinks a few bowls of rice wine or fermented coconut milk. Then he no longer feels his Self, he no longer feels the pain of life; he briefly finds numbness. Dozing off over his bowl of rice wine, he finds just the same thing that Siddhartha and Govinda find when they manage to flee their bodies with the help of lengthy exercises so as to linger in that-which-is-not-Self. This is how it is, Govinda."

Govinda replied, "So you say, O friend, and yet you know

that Siddhartha is no driver of oxen and a Samana is no drunk-ard. It is surely true that a drinker finds numbness, surely true that he briefly finds respite and escape, but then he returns from this delusion and finds all as it was. He has not grown wiser, has not gathered wisdom, has not ascended to a higher rung."

And Siddhartha, smiling, replied, "This I do not know; I have never been a drinker. But that I, Siddhartha, find numb-ness only briefly in my exercises and my *samadhi* and am just as far removed from wisdom, from redemption, as when I was a child in my mother's womb, this I do know, Govinda, and know it well."

On yet another occasion, as Siddhartha was leaving the forest with Govinda to beg sustenance for their brothers and teachers in the village, he began to speak.

"And now, Govinda, do you think we are on the right path? Are we drawing closer to knowledge? Are we drawing closer to redemption? Or are we not perhaps walking in circles—we who had hoped to escape the cycle?"

Govinda replied, "We have learned much, Siddhartha, and much remains to be learned. We are not walking in a circle, we are ascending; the circle is a spiral, and we have already climbed many of its steps."

Now Siddhartha asked, "How old, would you say, is the el-dest Samana among us, our venerable teacher?"

Govinda replied, "The eldest among us is perhaps sixty years of age."

And Siddhartha said, "So he has lived for sixty years and has not yet reached Nirvana. He will turn seventy and eighty, and you and I, we too will grow old and will continue to perform the exercises, to meditate and fast. But Nirvana will remain out of reach, both for him and for us. O Govinda, it seems to me that of all the Samanas that exist, there is perhaps not one, not a single one, who will reach Nirvana. We find consolations, we find numbness, we learn skills with which to deceive ourselves. But the essential, the Path of Paths, this we do not find."

"If only," Govinda said, "if only you would not utter such terrifying words, Siddhartha! How is it possible that among so many learned men, among so many Brahmins, among so many rigorous and venerable Samanas, among so many seekers, so many who are so deeply devoted, so many holy men, none should find the Path of Paths?"

But Siddhartha, in a voice that held as much sorrow as derision, a soft voice that was in part sad, in part mocking, said, "Soon, Govinda, your friend will leave behind this path of the Samanas that he has traveled so long at your side. I am suffering from thirst, Govinda, and upon this long Samana path I have found nothing to slake it. Always I have thirsted for knowledge, always been filled with questions. Year after year I questioned the Brahmins, year after year questioned the holy Vedas. Perhaps, O Govinda, it would have been just as well, just as clever and just as salutary, had I put my questions to the rhinoceros bird or the chimpanzee. It has taken me long to learn this, Govinda, and still I am not quite done learning it: that nothing can be learned! There is in fact—and this I believe—no such thing as what we call 'learning.' There is, my friend, only knowing, and this is everywhere; it is Atman, it is in me and in you and in every creature. And so I am beginning to believe that this knowing has no worse enemy than the desire to know, than learning itself."

Govinda stopped short in the middle of the road, raised his hands, and said, "If only, Siddhartha, you would not frighten your friend with such speeches! Truly, your words awaken fear in my heart. Consider: What would remain of the holiness of prayer, what of the venerability of the class of Brahmins, what of the holiness of the Samanas, if things were as you say, if there were no learning? What, O Siddhartha, would then become of all that is holy on earth, all that has value and is venerable?"

And Govinda murmured a verse under his breath, a verse from an Upanishad:

> "He who immerses himself in Atman, pondering
>   with pure spirit—
> The joy of his heart cannot be expressed in words."

Siddhartha was silent. He was thinking of the words Govinda had spoken, thinking them through to their conclusion.

Yes, he thought, standing with bowed head, what would remain of all that appeared holy to us? What does remain? What is proving to have lasting value? And he shook his head.

One day when the two youths had lived among the Samanas for nearly three years and shared their exercises, word reached them in a roundabout way, a rumor, a legend: A man had been discovered, by the name of Gautama, the Sublime One, the Buddha, who had overcome the sufferings of the world within himself and brought the wheel of rebirths to a halt. He was journeying through the countryside as an itinerant teacher, surrounded by disciples, without possessions, without a home, without womenfolk, dressed in the yellow cloak of an ascetic but with joyful brow, a Blessed One, and Brahmins and princes bowed down before him and became his pupils.

This legend, this rumor, this myth rippled and wafted through the air; in the towns all the Brahmins were speaking of it, in the forest the Samanas. Again and again the youths heard the name of Gautama, the Buddha, uttered by supporters and detractors alike, in both praise and vituperation.

Just as when, in a land devastated by plague, word begins to spread that in such and such a place there is a man, a wise man, a holder of knowledge, whose very word and breath have the power to cure the afflicted—just as this rumor then circulates through the countryside and everyone speaks of it, many believe it, many are doubtful, but many others set out at once in search of this wise man, this helper—in just such a way did this wafting legend of Gautama, the Buddha, the wise man from the race of the Sakya, make its way across the land. This man, his believers insisted, was possessed of the highest knowledge: He could remember his past lives; he had attained Nirvana and would never again return to the cycle, would never again have to dive into the murky stream of new shapes. Many splendid, incredible things were said of him: He had performed miracles, had vanquished the devil, had spoken with the gods. But his enemies and those who did not believe in him said that this Gautama was a vain seducer who lived a life of luxury and scoffed at sacrifices, who was devoid of learning and knew neither exercises nor self-castigation.

How sweet it sounded, this legend of the Buddha; enchantment wafted from the reports. The world, after all, was diseased, life difficult to bear, and lo! Here was a new spring bubbling up, a messenger's cry ringing out, consoling and mild, full of noble promises. Everywhere the rumor of the Buddha could be heard; everywhere in the lands of India youths pricked up their ears and were filled with longing, with hope; and among the Brahmins' sons in the villages and towns every pilgrim and stranger was welcome who brought news of him, the Sublime One, the Sakyamuni.

Even to the Samanas in the forest, even to Siddhartha, even to Govinda the legend had made its way, bit by bit, in drops, each drop heavy with hope, each drop heavy with doubt. It was not much spoken of, for the eldest of the Samanas was not well disposed to it. He had heard that this alleged Buddha had once been an ascetic and lived in the forest

but had then returned to a life of luxury and worldly pleasure; he did not think much of this Gautama.

"O Siddhartha," Govinda said one day to his friend, "today
I was in the village, and a Brahmin invited me to enter his
home, and in his home was a Brahmin's son from Magadha
who had seen the Buddha with his own eyes and heard his
doctrine. Truly, my chest ached with each breath, and I
thought to myself, If only the hour would come when I as
well, when the two of us, Siddhartha and I, might hear the
doctrine from the lips of that Perfect One! Speak, friend.
Should not we too go to that place and hear the doctrine from
the lips of the Buddha?"

Said Siddhartha, "I always thought, O Govinda, that
Govinda would remain among the Samanas, always believed
it was his goal to reach the age of sixty and seventy and still to
perform the arts and exercises that are the glory of Samana
existence. But it appears I knew Govinda too little, knew too
little of his heart. And so now, dearest friend, you wish to take
up a new path and go to the place where the Buddha is
preaching his doctrine."

Govinda replied, "Siddhartha is mocking me. Very well,
mock as you please! But has the desire, the longing to hear
this doctrine, not been awakened in you as well? And did you
not once say to me that you would not continue to walk the
path of the Samanas much longer?"

At this Siddhartha laughed after his own fashion, the tone of
his voice displaying both a hint of sorrow and a hint of derision, and said, "Well you have spoken, Govinda, quite well, and
remembered well, too. May you also remember what else you
have heard from me: namely, that I have become distrustful
and weary of doctrines and learning and that I have little faith
in words that come to us from teachers. But be that as it may,
dear friend, I am prepared to hear these teachings, though in
my heart I believe we have already tasted their finest fruit."

Said Govinda, "Your willingness delights my heart. But tell me, how can this be? How can it be that the teachings of Gautama have already offered up to us their finest fruit even before we have heard them?"

Siddhartha replied, "Let us enjoy this fruit, Govinda, and wait to see what will follow it! As for the fruit that Gautama has already given us, it is this: that he is calling us away from the Samanas! Whether he has other things as well to offer us, better ones—let us wait to discover this, my friend, with peace in our hearts."

That very day, Siddhartha informed the eldest Samana of his decision, saying that he wished to leave. He spoke with the courtesy and modesty befitting a younger man and pupil. The Samana, however, was filled with anger at the thought that these two youths wished to leave him; he raised his voice and used coarse, abusive language.

Govinda was horrified and filled with embarrassment. Siddhartha, however, put his mouth to Govinda's ear and whispered, "Now I'll show the old man what I learned as his pupil."

Stationing himself immediately before the Samana, his soul collected, he caught the eye of the old man with his own eyes and bewitched him, made him fall silent, made him lose his will, subjected him to his own will, commanded him to perform mutely what was asked of him. The old man fell silent: His eyes were locked in position, his will was paralyzed, his arms dangled down, he was powerless in the grasp of Siddhartha's enchantment. Now Siddhartha's thoughts took control of the thoughts of the Samana, forcing him to perform what they commanded. And so the old man bowed several times, made gestures of blessing, and, in a stammer, wished them safe travels. The youths responded to his bows with thanks, responded to his good wishes with wishes of their own, took their leave of him, and set off.

As they walked, Govinda said, "O Siddhartha, you learned more among the Samanas than I knew. It is difficult, very difficult, to enchant an old Samana. Verily, if you had remained there among them, you would soon have learned to walk upon water!"

"I do not wish to walk upon water," Siddhartha replied. "Let elderly Samanas content themselves with such tricks."

GAUTAMA

In the town of Savathi, every child knew the name of the Sublime Buddha, and every house was equipped to fill the alms bowls of Gautama's disciples, the silent mendicants. Not far from the town lay Gautama's preferred residence, Jetavana Grove, which the wealthy merchant Anathapindika, a devoted admirer of the Sublime One, had given to him and his followers.

This was the place mentioned in all the tales that had been shared with the two young ascetics in their search to discover Gautama's whereabouts, in all the answers they had received to their queries. And when they arrived in Savathi, they were offered food at the very first house at whose door they stopped to beg, and they accepted it.

Siddhartha asked the woman who gave it to them, "O charitable woman, we very much desire to learn where the Buddha can be found, the Most Venerable One, for we are two Samanas from the forest who have come here to see him, the Perfect One, and to hear his doctrine from his lips."

The woman replied, "Truly you have chosen the right place to stop, O Samanas from the forest. Jetavana, the garden of Anathapindika, is where the Sublime One resides. There, as pilgrims, you will be allowed to pass the night, for there is room in this place for the countless hordes who arrive in streams to hear the doctrine from his lips."

At these words, Govinda was glad and he cried out gaily, "How wonderful! Then our goal has been reached and our journey come to an end! But tell us, O mother of all pilgrims, do you know the Buddha? Have you beheld him with your own eyes?"

Said the woman, "I have seen him many times, the Sublime One. Many days I have seen him walking silently through our streets wearing his yellow coat, silently holding out his alms bowl at the doors of our homes and carrying the filled bowl away with him."

Govinda listened, rapt, and wanted to ask and hear much more. But Siddhartha announced it was time they were on their way. They gave their thanks and walked on, scarcely needing to inquire which way to go, for there were any number of pilgrims and monks from Gautama's fellowship on their way to Jetavana. And as they reached it that night, they beheld a scene of constant arrival, with the cries and conversations of those requesting and finding quarters. The two Samanas, accustomed to life in the forest, quickly and silently found shelter and rested there until morning.

When the sun rose, they were astonished to see what a great crowd of believers and onlookers had spent the night here. On all the paths of the splendid grove, monks were strolling in their yellow robes; they sat here and there beneath the trees, absorbed in contemplation or in spiritual conversation, the shady gardens like a city to behold, full of people swarming like bees. Most of these monks were setting out with their alms bowls to collect food in town for their noonday meal, the one meal of the day. Even the Buddha himself, the Enlightened One, was in the habit of going to beg for food each morning.

Siddhartha saw him and recognized him at once, as if a god had pointed him out: a simple man in a yellow cowl, walking quietly, alms bowl in his hand.

"Look!" Siddhartha said softly to Govinda. "That one there is the Buddha."

Attentively Govinda regarded the monk in the yellow cowl, who at first appeared indistinguishable from the hundreds of others. But Govinda, too, soon saw that this was indeed the Buddha, and they followed behind him, observing him.

The Buddha was walking along modestly, absorbed in thought. His still face was neither gay nor sad; he appeared to be smiling inwardly. Quietly, calmly, with a hidden smile, looking rather like a healthy child, the Buddha strolled down the path, wearing his robe and placing his foot upon the earth exactly like all his monks, just as was dictated to them. But his face and gait, his quietly lowered gaze, his quietly dangling hand—and indeed each individual finger on his quietly dangling hand—spoke of peace, spoke perfection, sought nothing, imitated nothing, was gently breathing an imperishable calm, an imperishable light, an inviolate peace.

Thus did Gautama stroll toward the town to collect alms, and the two Samanas recognized him solely by his perfect calm, the stillness of his figure, in which there was no searching, no desire, no imitation, no effort to be discerned, only light and peace.

"Today we shall hear the doctrine from his lips," Govinda said.

Siddhartha gave no reply. He felt no great curiosity to hear this doctrine. He did not think it would teach him anything new; after all, he, like Govinda, had already heard the substance of the Buddha's teachings over and over again, if only from second- and thirdhand reports. Nonetheless he scruti-

nized Gautama's head, his shoulders, his feet, his quietly dangling hand, and it seemed to him that every joint of every finger on this hand was doctrine; it spoke, breathed, wafted, and
glinted Truth. This man, this Buddha, was genuine down to
the gestures of his littlest finger. This man was holy. Never
had Siddhartha revered a man like this, never had he loved a
man as he loved this one.

The two of them followed the Buddha into town and then
returned in silence, for they intended to abstain from food
that day. They saw Gautama return, saw him take his meal in
the circle of his disciples—what he ate would not have satisfied a bird—and saw him withdraw into the shade of the
mango trees.

And in the evening, when the day's heat had abated and
everyone around the camp came to life and gathered together,
they heard the Buddha teach. They heard his voice, and it too
was flawless, flawlessly calm and full of peace. Gautama
preached the doctrine of suffering, of the origins of suffering,
of the path to the cessation of suffering. His words flowed
quiet and clear. Suffering was life, the world was full of sorrow, but redemption from sorrow had been found: He who
trod the path of the Buddha would find redemption.

With a soft yet firm voice, the Sublime One spoke, preaching the four basic principles, preaching the eightfold path. Pa-
tiently he trod the familiar path of his doctrine, of the
examples, the repetitions, his high clear voice floating above
his listeners like a light, like a starry sky.

When the Buddha—night had already fallen—completed
his speech, a number of pilgrims stepped forward and asked
to be accepted into his fellowship; they wished to take refuge
in his doctrine. And Gautama took them in, saying, "You have
heard the doctrine; it has been preached to you. Join our
number, then, and walk in holiness, that an end may be put to
all sorrow."

And lo! Govinda too stepped forward, shy Govinda, and said, "I too take refuge in the Sublime One and his doctrine," and asked that he be taken in as a disciple, and he was taken in.

Directly afterward, when the Buddha had retired for the night, Govinda turned to Siddhartha and spoke earnestly. "Siddhartha, it is not fitting for me to reproach you. Both of us heard the Sublime One; both of us heard his teachings. Govinda heard the doctrine and has taken refuge in it. But you, my revered friend, will you not also tread the path of redemption? Must you hesitate, must you persist in waiting?"

Siddhartha awoke as if from slumber when he heard Govinda's words. For a long time he gazed into Govinda's face. Then he said softly, in a voice free of mockery, "Govinda, my friend, now you have taken the step, now you have chosen the path. Always, O Govinda, you have been my friend, and always you have walked one step behind me. Often I have thought, Will not Govinda one day take a step on his own without me, as his own soul commands? And behold, now you have become a man and are choosing your own path. May you follow it to its end, O my friend! May you find redemption!"

Govinda, who did not yet fully comprehend, repeated his question with a touch of impatience. "Tell me, I beg you, my friend! Tell me, as it cannot be otherwise, that you too, my learned companion, will take your refuge in the sublime Buddha!"

Siddhartha placed his hand on Govinda's shoulder. "You did not hear my blessing, Govinda. I shall repeat it: May you follow this path to its end! May you find redemption!"

At this moment Govinda realized that his friend had left him, and he began to weep. "Siddhartha!" he cried out mournfully.

Siddhartha said to him in a kind voice, "Do not forget, Govinda, that you now belong to the Samanas of the Buddha! You have renounced your birthplace and parents, renounced your origins and property, renounced your own will, re-nounced friendship. This is what the doctrine instructs; this is the will of the Sublime One and it is what you yourself have chosen. Tomorrow, Govinda, I shall take leave of you."

The friends continued their stroll through the coppice for a long time; for a long time they lay and could not find sleep. Again and again Govinda pressed his friend to tell him why he would not take refuge in Gautama's teachings, what errors he saw in his doctrine. But Siddhartha turned him away each time, saying, "Be satisfied, Govinda! The teachings of the Sublime One are excellent; how could I find an error in them?"

Very early the next morning, a follower of the Buddha, one of his oldest monks, walked through the garden summoning all the new arrivals who had taken refuge in the doctrine of the Buddha, so as to give them their yellow robes and instruct them in the first lessons and duties of their state. Govinda broke away from them, embraced the friend of his youth one last time, then joined the procession of novices.

Siddhartha wandered through the grove, deep in thought.

There he came upon Gautama, the Sublime One, and as he greeted him with reverence and found the gaze of the Buddha so full of kindness and peace, the youth plucked up the courage to ask the Venerable One's leave to address him. Silently the Sublime One nodded his consent.

Said Siddhartha, "Yesterday, O Sublime One, I had the privilege of hearing your marvelous teachings. Together with my friend I came from far away to hear this doctrine. And now my friend will remain among your followers; he has taken refuge in you, while I am once more embarking on my pil-grimage."

"As you please," the Sublime One said courteously.

"My words are all too bold," Siddhartha went on, "but I wish not to leave the Sublime One without having shared my thoughts with him frankly. Would the Venerable One honor me with his audience a moment longer?"

Silently the Buddha nodded his consent.

Said Siddhartha, "There is one thing in particular, O Most Venerable One, that I have admired in your teachings. Everything in your doctrine is utterly clear, is proven; you show the world as a perfect chain, a chain never and nowhere interrupted, an eternal chain forged of causes and effects. Never has this been so clearly beheld, never so irrefutably presented. In truth, it must make the heart of any Brahmin beat faster when, through your teachings, he is able to glimpse the world as a perfect continuum, free of gaps, clear as a crystal, not dependent on chance, not dependent on gods. Whether this world be good or evil, and life in it sorrow or joy—let us set this question aside, for it is quite possibly not essential. But the oneness of the world, the continuum of all occurrences, the enfolding of all things great and small within a single stream, a single law of causes, of becoming and of death, this shines brightly forth from your sublime doctrine, O Perfect One. But now, according to your very same doctrine, this oneness and logical consistency of all things is nevertheless interrupted at one point; there is a tiny hole through which something strange is flowing into this world of oneness, something new, something that wasn't there before and that cannot be shown and cannot be proven: This is your doctrine of the overcoming of the world, of redemption. With this tiny hole, this tiny gap, the entire eternal unified law of the world is smashed to pieces, rendered invalid. May you forgive me for giving voice to this objection."

Silently, Gautama had heard him out, unmoved. In his kind, courteous, and clear voice, the Perfect One now spoke. "You have heard my teachings, O Brahmin's son, and it is well for you that you have thought so deeply about them. You have found a gap in them, an error. May you continue to contemplate it. But allow me to warn you, O inquisitive one, about the thicket of opinions and quibbling over words. Opinions are of little account; be they lovely or displeasing, clever or foolish, anyone can subscribe to or dismiss them. But the doctrine you heard from me is not my opinion, and its goal is not to explain the world to the inquisitive. It has a different goal; its goal is redemption from suffering. It is this redemption Gautama teaches, nothing else."

"May you not be angry with me, O Sublime One," the youth replied. "It is not to quarrel, to quibble over words, that I spoke to you thus. Truly you are right; opinions are of little account. But let me say this as well: Never for a moment have I doubted you. I never doubted for a moment that you are the Buddha, that you have reached the goal, the highest goal, toward which so many thousands of Brahmins and Brahmins' sons are striving. You have found redemption from death. It came to you as you were engaged in a search of your own, upon a path of your own; it came to you through thinking, through meditation, through knowledge, through enlightenment. Not through doctrine did it come to you. And this is my thought, O Sublime One: No one will ever attain redemption through doctrine! Never, O Venerable One, will you be able to convey in words and show and say through your teachings what happened to you in the hour of your enlightenment. Much is contained in the doctrine of the enlightened Buddha; many are taught by it to live in an upright way, to shun evil. But there is one thing this so clear and venerable doctrine does not contain: It does not contain the secret of what the Sublime One himself experienced, he alone among the hundreds of thousands. This is what I thought and realized when I heard the doctrine. This is why I am continuing my journey—not in order to seek a different, better doctrine, for I know there is none, but to leave behind me all teachings and all teachers and to reach my goal alone or perish. But often will I remember this day, O Sublime One, and this hour when my eyes beheld a holy man."

The eyes of the Buddha gazed in stillness at the ground; his unfathomable face shone in stillness and perfect equanimity.

"May your thoughts," the Venerable One said slowly, "not be in error! May you reach your goal! But tell me: Have you seen the horde of Samanas, my many brothers, who have taken refuge in the doctrine? And do you believe, unknown Samana, do you believe they would all be better off if they abandoned the doctrine and returned to the life of the world and its pleasures?"

"Far be it from me to entertain such a thought!" Siddhartha cried. "May they all remain faithful to the doctrine, may they reach their goal! It is not fitting for me to pass judgment on another's life! Only for myself, for myself alone, must I judge, must I choose, must I reject. Redemption from Self is what we Samanas seek, O Sublime One. If I were one of your disciples, O Venerable One, what I fear might happen is that my Self would only apparently, deceptively find peace and be redeemed, but that in truth it would live on and become huge, for I would have made the doctrine and my adherence to it and my love for you and the fellowship of the monks my Self!"

With a half smile, with imperturbable brightness and amicability, Gautama looked directly into the face of the stranger and bade him farewell with a scarcely visible gesture.

"You are clever, O Samana," said the Venerable One. "You speak cleverly, my friend. Be on your guard against too much cleverness!"

The Buddha wandered off, but his gaze and his half smile remained forever engraved in Siddhartha's memory.

Never have I seen a man gaze and smile like this, sit and walk like this, he thought; I myself would like to be able to gaze and smile, sit and walk in just such a way, so freely, so venerably, so secretly, so openly, so childishly and mysteriously. Truly, only a man who has penetrated the innermost core of his being can gaze and walk like that. Very well, I too will seek to penetrate the innermost core of my being.

I have seen one man, thought Siddhartha, just a single man before whom I have had to cast down my eyes. I do not wish to cast my eyes down before another ever again. Never will I be tempted by any other doctrine, for the doctrine of this man did not tempt me.

The Buddha has robbed me, Siddhartha thought, he has robbed me, and yet he has given me so much more. He has robbed me of my friend, the friend who believed in me and now believes in him, who was my shadow and is now Gautama's shadow. But he has given me Siddhartha, given me myself.

Awakening

When Siddhartha left the grove in which the Buddha, the Perfect One, remained behind, in which Govinda remained behind, he felt that his former life, too, was remaining behind him in this grove. Immersed in deep contemplation of this feeling, which had taken hold of him completely, he walked slowly away, allowing himself to sink to the bottom of this feeling as if through deep water, down to where the causes lay. Recognizing the causes, it seemed to him, was just what thought was; it was only in this way that feelings gave rise to insights and, rather than being lost, took on substance and began to radiate what was within them.

Walking slowly away, Siddhartha realized he was a youth no longer; he had become a man. He realized that something had left him, the way a snake's old skin leaves it. Something that had accompanied him throughout his youth and been a part of him was no longer present: the desire to have teachers and hear doctrine. He had left behind the last teacher to appear to him on his path, this highest and wisest of teachers, the holiest one, Buddha; he'd had to part even from him, unable to accept his doctrine.

Thinking, he walked ever more slowly and asked himself, What is it now that you were hoping to learn from doctrines and teachers, and what is it that they—who taught you so much—were unable to teach you? And, he decided, It was the Self whose meaning and nature I wished to learn. It was the Self I wished to escape from, wished to overcome. But I was unable to overcome it, I could only trick it, could only run away from it and hide. Truly, not a single thing in all the world has so occupied my thoughts as this Self of mine, this riddle: that I am alive and that I am One, am different and separate from all others, that I am Siddhartha! And there is not a thing in the world about which I know less than about myself, about Siddhartha!

Gripped by this thought, the slowly walking thinker stopped short, and at once a further thought sprang from the first one, a thought that was new to him.

That I know nothing of myself, that Siddhartha has remained such a stranger to me, such an unknown, comes from one cause, from a single cause: I was afraid of myself, was running away from myself! I was searching for Atman, searching for Brahman; I was prepared to chop my ego into little pieces and peel off its layers so as to find, in its unknown innermost core, the kernel that lies at the heart of every husk: Atman, Life, the Divine, that final utmost thing. But I myself got lost in the process.

Siddhartha raised his eyes and looked about. A smile filled his face, and a profound sense of awakening from a long dream coursed through him down to his toes. At once he began to walk again, now taking hurried steps like a man who knows what he must do.

Oh, he thought, breathing a deep sigh of relief, I won't let Siddhartha slip away from me again. I won't let my life and my thought begin with Atman and the world's sorrows. No more killing myself, no more chopping myself into bits in the hope of finding some secret hidden among the debris. I will no longer follow Yoga-Veda, or Atharva-Veda, or the ascetics, or any other doctrine. I'll be my own teacher, my own pupil. I'll study myself, learn the secret that is Siddhartha.

He looked around as if seeing the world for the first time. How beautiful it was, how colorful, how strange and mysterious! Here was blue, here was yellow, here was green; sky and river were flowing; forests and mountains stood fixed: Everything was beautiful, everything mysterious and magical, and in the midst of all this was he, Siddhartha, in the moment of his awakening, on the path to himself. All these things, all this yellow and blue, river and forest, passed through Siddhartha's eye and entered him for the first time; they were no longer the illusion of Mara, no longer the veil of Maya, no longer the meaningless random multiplicity of the world of appearances, contemptible to any deep thinker among Brahmins, any thinker who scoffed at multiplicity and sought oneness. Blue was blue, river was river, and even if the One, the Divine, lay hidden in the blue and the river within Siddhartha, it was still the nature and intention of the Divine to be yellow here, blue here, sky over there, forest there, and here Siddhartha. Meaning and being did not lie somewhere behind things; they lay within them, within everything.

How deaf I have been, how unfeeling! he thought, walking ever more swiftly. When a person reads something and wishes to grasp its meaning, he does not scorn the characters and letters and call them illusory, random, and worthless husks; he reads them, studies them, and loves them, letter for letter. But I—I who set out to read the book of the world and the book of my own being—I scorned the characters and letters in deference to a meaning I assumed in advance, I called the world of appearances illusory, called my own eye and my own tongue random and worthless illusions. Enough of all this. I have awoken, have truly awoken, and this day is the day of my birth.

As Siddhartha was thinking this thought, he stopped short once more, as though a snake were lying on the path before him.

For all at once this too had dawned on him: He, who truly was like a person freshly awakened or like a newborn, would have to begin his life anew, starting from nothing. When he had departed from Jetavana Grove this morning, the grove of the Sublime One, already awakening, already on the path to himself, it had been his intention and had appeared to him only natural, a matter of course, to return to the place of his birth and his father now that his years as an ascetic had ended. But just at the moment when he stopped short, as though a snake were lying across his path, he awoke also to this insight: I am no longer who I was; I am no longer an ascetic, I am no longer a priest, I am no longer a Brahmin. What would I do at home with my father, study? Sacrifice? Practice *samadhi*? All these things are now over; they no longer lie along my path.

Motionless, Siddhartha remained standing there, and for a moment, for the space of a single breath, his heart was freezing cold; he could feel it freezing in his breast like a small animal, a bird or a rabbit, when he saw how alone he was. For years he had been without a home and had not felt it. Now he felt it. Always, even in the most distant depths of *samadhi,* he had been his father's son, a Brahmin, a person of high birth, a thinker. Now he was no longer anything but Siddhartha; he was the one who had awoken and nothing more. He drew in a deep breath and for a moment he shivered, freezing. No one was as alone as he was. Every nobleman had his place among noblemen, every craftsman had his place among craftsmen and found refuge with them, sharing their life and speaking in their tongue. Every Brahmin belonged among Brahmins and lived with them. Every ascetic could find refuge among the Samanas. Even the most obscure hermit in the forest was not utterly alone; he too was enfolded in belonging, he too belonged to a class that was his home. Govinda had become a monk, and a thousand monks were his brothers, wore his habit, believed his beliefs, spoke his tongue. But he, Siddhartha: Where did he belong? Whose life would he share? Whose tongue would he speak?

From this moment when the world around him melted away and left him as solitary as a star in the sky, from this moment of cold and despondency, Siddhartha emerged, more firmly Self than before, solidified. This, he felt, had been the final shiver of awakening, the final pangs of birth. And at once he began to walk again, striding quickly and impatiently, no longer in the direction of home, no longer toward his father, no longer back.

PART TWO

Dedicated to Wilhelm Gundert,
my cousin in Japan

KAMALA

Siddhartha learned new things with every step along his path, for the world was transformed and his heart was enchanted. He watched the sun rise above wooded mountains and set above the distant palm-lined shore. At night he saw the stars arranged in formation on the sky and the crescent moon drifting like a boat on a sea of blue. He saw trees, stars, animals, clouds, rainbows, cliffs, herbs and flowers, stream and river, the flash of dew in morning bushes, distant high mountains blue and pale; birds were singing, so were bees, and wind blew silvery through the rice paddies. All these things, various and many-hued, had always been there—the sun and moon had always shone, rivers had always rushed, and bees had always buzzed—but all of it had formerly been nothing for Siddhartha but a fleeting, deceptive veil before his eyes, to be regarded with distrust, penetrated by thought, and destroyed, since it was not true Being: Being lay beyond the visible. But now his liberated eye dwelled in this realm, saw and recognized the visible, and was searching for a home in this world; no longer was it in search of Being, no longer were its efforts directed toward the Beyond. How beautiful the world was when one looked at it without searching, just looked, simply and innocently. How lovely the moon and stars were, how lovely the stream and its bank, forest and cliff, nanny goat and jewel beetle, flower and butterfly. How beautiful, how lovely it was to walk through the world like this, like a child, so awake, so open to what was near at hand, so free of distrust. The sun burned differently upon his head, the shade of the forest cooled him differently, stream and cistern tasted different, different were the flavors of pumpkin and banana. The days were brief; the nights were brief. Each hour flew quickly past like a sail upon the sea, and beneath this sail lay a ship filled with treasures, filled with joys. Siddhartha saw a band of monkeys traveling in the high-up vault of the forest, in the uppermost branches, and heard a wild, lustful singing. Siddhartha saw a ram pursue a ewe and mate with her. In a lake thick with reeds he saw a pike hunting to still his evening hunger. Entire schools of young fish shot anxiously out of the water before him, flickering and flashing; strength and passion scented the air above the urgent whirlpools this indefatigable hunter left in his wake.

All these things had always been there, and yet he had not seen them; he had not been present. Now he was present, he belonged. Light and shade passed through his eyes, star and moon passed through his heart.

As he walked, Siddhartha also thought back on everything he had experienced in the garden of Jetavana: the doctrine he had heard there, the divine Buddha, bidding farewell to Govinda, his conversation with the Sublime One. He thought back on the words he had spoken to the Sublime One, on each of them, and with astonishment he realized he had said things that he had not yet really known. What he had said to Gautama—that his, the Buddha's, treasure and secret was not his doctrine but rather the inexpressible, unteachable things he had experienced in the hour of his enlightenment—was precisely what he, Siddhartha, was now setting off to experience, was now beginning to experience. It was he himself he now had to experience. To be sure, he had known for a long time that his Self was Atman, of the same eternal essence as Brahman. But never had he truly found this Self, for he had been trying to capture it with a net made of thought. While certainly body was not Self—nor was it the play of the senses— this Self was also not thought, was not mind, was not the wisdom amassed through learning, not the learned art of drawing conclusions and spinning new thoughts out of old. No, even thought was still in this world; no goal could be reached by killing off the happenstance Self of the senses while continuing to fatten the happenstance Self of thought and learnedness. Thought and senses were both fine things. Ultimate meaning lay hidden behind them; both should be listened to, played with, neither scorned nor overvalued, for in each of them the secret voice of the innermost core might be discerned. He would aspire to nothing but what this voice commanded him, occupy himself with nothing but what the voice advised. Why had Gautama once, in the hour of hours, sat down beneath the bo tree where enlightenment struck him? He had heard a voice, a voice in his own heart, commanding him to rest beneath this tree, and he had not chosen to devote himself instead to self-castigation, sacrifice, ablution, or prayer, nor to eating or drinking, nor to sleeping or dreaming; he had obeyed the voice. To obey like this, to obey not a command from the outside but only the voice, to be in readiness—this was good, this was necessary. Nothing else was necessary.

During the night as he slept in the straw hut of a ferryman beside the river, Siddhartha had a dream. Govinda was standing before him clad in the yellow robe of an ascetic. He looked sad, and sadly he asked, Why have you forsaken me? Siddhartha embraced Govinda, he flung his arms about him, but when he drew him to his breast and kissed him, it was no longer Govinda he held but a woman, and beneath the woman's robe a full breast was swelling. Siddhartha lay at this breast and drank; sweet and strong was the taste of this breast milk. It tasted of woman and man, of sun and forest, of animal and flower, of every fruit and every pleasure. It made him drunk, robbed him of his senses.... When Siddhartha awoke, the pale river was shimmering through the doorway of the hut, and from the forest came the dark hoot of an owl, deep and melodious.

At daybreak, Siddhartha asked his host, the ferryman, to take him across the river. The ferryman took him across the river on his bamboo raft; the broad expanse of water shimmered red in the dawn light.

"The river is beautiful," he said to his companion.

"Yes," the ferryman said, "it is a very beautiful river. I love it above all else. Often I have listened to it, often gazed into its eyes, and always I have learned from it. You can learn a great deal from a river."

"I thank you, my benefactor," Siddhartha said, stepping onto the opposite bank. "I have no gift to give you, dear friend, no wages to pay. I am a man without a home, a Brahmin's son and Samana."

"This I saw myself," said the ferryman, "and I expected neither payment nor gift from you. You will give me a gift some other time."

"Do you think so?" Siddhartha asked, amused.

"Certainly. This too I have learned from the river: Everything comes back again! You too, Samana, will come back again. And now farewell! May your friendship be my wages. May you remember me when you are sacrificing to the gods."

Smiling, they parted. Smiling, Siddhartha felt happiness at the friendship and friendliness of the ferryman. He is like Govinda, he thought, smiling. All the people I meet upon my way are like Govinda. All of them are grateful, though they themselves have cause to expect gratitude. All of them are deferential, all are eager to be a friend, to obey and think little. People are children.

Around noon he passed through a village. In front of the mud huts, children were rolling about in the street, playing with pumpkin seeds and shells, shouting and scrapping, but all of them ran away, shy before the unknown Samana. At the end of the village the path led through a stream, and at the edge of the stream a young woman knelt, washing clothes. When Siddhartha greeted her, she raised her head and looked up at him with a smile that made the whites of her eyes flash. He called out a blessing to her, as is customary among travelers, and asked how much farther it was to the city. She stood up and came over to him, her moist lips shimmering and beautiful in her young face. She engaged him in banter, asking if he had eaten yet and if it was true that the Samanas slept alone in the forest at night and were not allowed to have women with them. As she spoke, she placed her left foot upon his right and made the gesture a woman makes when she is inviting a man to indulge in the sort of love pleasure the instructional books call "climbing the tree." Siddhartha felt his blood grow warm, and as his dream returned to him at this moment, he bent down before the woman and kissed the brown tip of her breast. Looking up, he saw desire in her smiling face, and her half-closed eyes beseeched him longingly.

Siddhartha too was filled with longing and felt the source of his sex stir, but as he had never before touched a woman, he hesitated for a moment while his hands were already preparing to reach out for her. And in this moment he heard something that made him tremble: It was his inner voice, and the voice said no. At once the charm vanished from the smiling face of the young woman; all he saw now was the dewy gaze of a beast in heat. With a friendly gesture he stroked her cheek, turned away from her, and with a light step disappeared into the bamboo thicket, leaving the disappointed woman behind.

Before evening he came to a large city and was happy, for he felt the desire to be among people. He'd lived a long time in the forest, and the straw hut of the ferryman in which he'd spent the night was the first roof he'd had over his head in quite a while.

Just outside the city, near a lovely fenced-in grove, the wanderer encountered a small company of maids and menservants laden with baskets. In their midst, an ornate sedan chair with four bearers held a woman seated upon red cushions beneath a brightly colored canopy: their mistress. Siddhartha remained standing at the entrance to the pleasure garden and observed this procession; saw the servants, the maids, the baskets, the sedan chair, and the lady seated in it. Beneath black hair piled high upon her head, he saw a very fair, very delicate, very clever face, a bright red mouth like a fig split in two, eyebrows groomed and painted in high arches, dark eyes clever and watchful, a long pale throat rising out of a green and gold outer garment, fair hands in repose, long and narrow, with thick golden bracelets about the wrists.

Siddhartha saw how beautiful she was, and his heart rejoiced. Deeply he bowed before her as the sedan chair approached, and as he straightened up again he looked into her pale, lovely face, read for a moment her clever eyes beneath their high arches, caught a whiff of a perfume he did not know. Smiling, the beautiful woman nodded, just for an instant; then she disappeared into the grove with her servants behind her.

Siddhartha thought, What a fine omen marks my arrival in this city! He felt an urge to hurry into the grove straightaway but then thought better of it; only now did it occur to him how the servants and maids standing at its entrance had looked at him, with what contempt, what suspicion, what displeasure.

Even now, I am a Samana, he thought, an ascetic and men- dicant. I will not be able to remain as I am, will not be able to enter the grove in this guise. He gave a laugh.

He asked the next person to come along what this grove was and the name of the woman, and learned that this was the grove of Kamala, the famous courtesan, and that in addition to the grove she owned a house in town.

Then he entered the city. He now had a goal.

In pursuit of this goal, he allowed the city to suck him in, drifted with the current down its streets, paused in its squares, rested upon the stone steps along the river. Toward evening he made the acquaintance of a barber's assistant he had ob- served working in the shadow of an archway and encountered again praying in a temple of Vishnu; he regaled him with tales of Vishnu and Lakshmi. He slept that night beside the river where the boats were moored, and early the next morning, before the first customers arrived at the shop, he had the bar- ber's assistant shave off his beard, cut and comb his hair, and anoint it with precious oil. Then he went to the river to bathe.

When, late in the afternoon, the beautiful Kamala ap- proached her grove in her sedan chair, Siddhartha was stand- ing at the entrance; he bowed and received the courtesan's greeting. Then he signaled to the last of the servants follow- ing in her train and asked him to tell his mistress a young Brahmin wished to speak with her. After a while the servant returned and instructed the waiting youth to follow him; without another word, he led Siddhartha to a pavilion where Kamala was reclining upon a daybed and left him alone with her.

"Was it not you standing there yesterday greeting me?" Kamala asked.

"Yes, I saw you yesterday and greeted you."

"But did you not have a beard yesterday, and long hair, and dust in your hair?"

"You certainly observed well, seeing all this. You saw Siddhartha, the Brahmin's son, who left home to become a Samana and was a Samana for three years. But now I have left that path behind me and come to this city, and the first person I saw here, even before entering the city, was you. I have come here to tell you this, O Kamala! You are the first woman to whom Siddhartha has spoken without averting his eyes. Never again shall I avert my eyes when I meet a beautiful woman."

Kamala smiled and played with her fan of peacock feathers. "And is it only to tell me this that Siddhartha has come?" she asked.

"To tell you this, and to thank you for being so beautiful. And if it does not displease you, Kamala, I would like to ask you to be my friend and teacher, for I know nothing of the art of which you are a master."

At this Kamala laughed aloud. "Never before, my friend, has a Samana come out of the forest and asked to learn from me. Never has a Samana with long hair and clad in a torn loincloth paid me a visit. Many young men come to call on me—there are even Brahmins' sons among them—but they come in beautiful clothes, they come in fine shoes, and they have fragrance in their hair and money in their wallets. This, O Samana, is what the young men are like who come to call on me."

Siddhartha said, "Already I am beginning to learn from you. Even yesterday I learned something. Already I have given up my beard and combed and oiled my hair. Very little is still lacking, most splendid woman: fine clothes, fine shoes, money in my wallet. Know that Siddhartha has undertaken far more difficult tasks than these and has succeeded in them. How could I fail to succeed in yesterday's resolve: to be your friend and learn from you the pleasures of love? You will find me a willing pupil, Kamala; I have learned more difficult things than what you are to teach me. So tell me: Is Siddhartha satisfactory to you as he is now, with oil in his hair but without clothes, shoes, or money?"

Laughing, Kamala cried out, "No, cherished friend, he is not yet satisfactory. He must have clothes, attractive clothes, and shoes, attractive shoes, and plenty of money in his wallet, and presents for Kamala. Now do you understand, Samana from the forest? Will you remember?"

"Certainly I shall remember," Siddhartha cried. "How could I fail to remember words that come from such lips? Your mouth is like a fig split in two, Kamala. My mouth, too, is fresh and red; it will fit nicely against yours, you'll see. But tell me, beautiful Kamala, are you not at all afraid of this Samana from the forest who has come to learn the art of love?"

"Why should I be afraid of a Samana, a foolish Samana from the forest who has been living among the jackals and doesn't even know yet what a woman is?"

"Oh, but he is strong, this Samana, and he is afraid of nothing. He could force you, beautiful girl. He could carry you off. He could harm you."

"No, Samana, I have no fear of this. Has a Samana or a Brahmin ever been afraid that someone might come and seize him and rob him of his learnedness, his piousness, and his profound thoughts? No, for these things belong to him, and he gives of them only what and to whom he will. It is precisely the same with Kamala and the pleasures of love. Beautiful and red is Kamala's mouth, but try to kiss it against her will and you will get from it not a single drop of sweetness, though it has much sweetness to offer. You are a willing pupil, Siddhartha, so learn this as well: Love can be begged, bought, or received as a gift, one can find it in the street, but one cannot steal it. This notion of yours is misguided. It would be a shame if a handsome youth like you were to set about things in the wrong way."

Siddhartha bowed to her, smiling. "A shame it would be, Kamala, how right you are! A terrible shame. No, not a single drop of your mouth's sweetness shall go to waste, and you will taste the full sweetness of mine. Let this be our agreement: Siddhartha will come again when he has what he is presently lacking: clothes, shoes, and money. But tell me, lovely Kamala, can you not give me one more piece of advice?"

"Advice? Why not? Who would refuse advice to a poor, ignorant Samana who has come from the jackals of the forest?"

"Advise me then, dear Kamala: Where should I go to find these three things the most swiftly?"

"Friend, that is something many would like to know. You must do what you have learned to do and in exchange have people give you money and clothes and shoes. There is no other way for a poor man to get money. What do you know how to do?"

"I can think. I can wait. I can fast."

"Is that all?"

"Yes ... no. I can also compose poetry. Would you give me a kiss for a poem?"

"If the poem pleases me, then yes. What is it called?"

Siddhartha reflected for a moment, then spoke these lines:

"Into her shady grove stepped beautiful Kamala,
  At the entrance to the grove stood the brown Samana.
  Deeply he bowed, having glimpsed the lotus blossom,
  for which he was thanked by smiling Kamala.
  More lovely, thought the youth, than sacrificing to the gods,
  More lovely it is to sacrifice to beautiful Kamala."

Kamala clapped her hands loudly, making the golden bracelets ring out.

"How beautiful your poetry is, brown Samana! Truly, I will be losing nothing if I trade you a kiss for it."

She drew him to her with her eyes; he lowered his face to

hers and placed his mouth upon the mouth that was like a fig split in two. For a long time Kamala kissed him, and with deep astonishment Siddhartha felt how she was teaching him, how wise she was, how she mastered him, pushed him away, lured him, and how behind this first kiss stood a long, well-ordered, and well-tried sequence of kisses, each different from the others, still awaiting him. Breathing deeply, he stood there and in this moment was like a child, gaping in astonishment at the wealth of things worth knowing and learning that had opened before his eyes.

"How very beautiful your poetry is!" Kamala exclaimed. "If I were rich, I would give you pieces of gold for it. But it will be difficult for you to earn as much money as you need with poetry. For you will need a great deal of money if you wish to be Kamala's friend."

"How you can kiss, Kamala!" Siddhartha stammered.

"Yes, I kiss well, and therefore I am not lacking in clothes, shoes, bracelets, or any other beautiful things. But what will become of you? Can you do nothing besides think, fast, and write poems?"

"I know the sacrificial songs," Siddhartha said, "but I don't want to sing them any longer. I know magical incantations, but I don't want to utter them any longer. I have read the writings of—"

"Stop." Kamala interrupted him. "You can read and write?"

"Certainly I can. Many can do these things."

"Most cannot. Even I cannot. It is very good that you can read and write, very good. And the incantations will be of use to you as well."

At this moment a maidservant ran in to the pavilion and whispered something in her mistress's ear.

"I must receive a guest," Kamala cried. "Hurry and get out of sight, Siddhartha. No one may see you here, remember that! Tomorrow I will receive you again."

She instructed the maid to give the pious Brahmin a white cloak. Before he knew what was happening, Siddhartha found himself whisked away by the maid and taken by a circuitous route to a garden house, where he was given a cloak. Then he was led into the bushes and urgently admonished to find his way out of the grove at once and unseen.

Pleased with himself, he did as he was told. Being accustomed to life in the forest, he was able to find his way out of the grove and over the hedge without a sound. Pleased with himself, he returned to the city, carrying the rolled-up cloak beneath his arm. In a hostel where travelers stopped, he positioned himself at the door, silently asked for food, silently accepted a piece of rice cake. Perhaps as soon as tomorrow, he thought, I will no longer be asking for food.

Pride suddenly flared up within him. He was no longer a Samana, no longer was it fitting for him to beg. He gave the rice cake to a dog and went without eating.

Simple is the life one leads here in the world, Siddhartha thought. There are no difficulties. Everything was difficult, laborious, and in the end hopeless when I was still a Samana. Now everything is easy, easy as the kissing lessons Kamala is giving me. I need clothing and money, that is all. These goals are small and within reach; they will not trouble my sleep.

He had long since identified Kamala's town house, and the next day he presented himself there.

"All is well," she cried out when she saw him. "You are expected at the home of Kamaswami; he is the richest merchant in the city. If you please him, he will take you into his service. Be clever, brown Samana. I have had others tell him of you. Be friendly toward him; he is very powerful. But do not be too modest! I do not want you to become his servant. You must become his equal, otherwise I shall not be satisfied with you. Kamaswami is beginning to grow old and lazy. If you please him, he will entrust you with a great deal."

Siddhartha thanked her and laughed, and when she learned that he had eaten nothing this day or the one before, she ordered bread and fruit to be brought and served him herself.

"You've been lucky," she said, as he was taking leave of her. "One door after the other is opening before you. How is that? Do you have magical powers?"

Siddhartha said, "Yesterday I told you that I knew how to think, to wait, and to fast, but you declared these things to have no value. But they have great value, Kamala, as you will see. You will see that the foolish Samanas in the forest learn and are able to do many fine things that you cannot. The day before yesterday I was still an unkempt beggar, but already yesterday I kissed Kamala, and soon I shall be a merchant and have money and all these things you consider important."

"Well, yes," she conceded, "but where would you be without me? What would you be if Kamala did not help you?"

"Dear Kamala," said Siddhartha, straightening up to his full height, "when I came into your grove to you, I was taking my first step. It was my resolve to learn love from this most beautiful of women. From the moment I resolved to do this, I knew I would succeed. I knew you would help me; from the first glance you gave me at the entrance to the grove I knew this."

"And if I hadn't been willing?"

"You *were* willing. You see, Kamala, when you throw a stone into the water, it hurries by the swiftest possible path to the bottom. It is like this when Siddhartha has a goal, a resolve. Siddhartha does nothing—he waits, he thinks, he fasts—but he passes through the things of this world like a stone through water, without doing anything, without moving; he is drawn and lets himself fall. His goal draws him to it, for he allows nothing into his soul that might conflict with this goal. This is what Siddhartha learned among the Samanas. It is what fools call magic and think is performed by demons.

Nothing is performed by demons; there are no demons. Anyone can perform magic. Anyone can reach his goals if he can think, if he can wait, if he can fast."

Kamala listened to him. She loved his voice, she loved the way his eyes flashed. "Perhaps it is just as you say, friend," she said softly. "But perhaps it is also that Siddhartha is a handsome man, his appearance is pleasing to women, and for this reason good luck comes to him."

With a kiss, Siddhartha took leave of her. "May it be so, my teacher. May my appearance always please you; may good luck always come from you to me!"

AMONG THE CHILD PEOPLE

Siddhartha went to see the merchant Kamaswami and was shown into a mansion; servants led him between precious tapestries to a chamber, where he waited for the master of the house to appear.

Kamaswami entered, a quick, agile man with heavily graying hair, very clever, cautious eyes, and a covetous mouth. Master and guest exchanged a friendly greeting.

"They tell me," the merchant began, "that you are a Brahmin, a learned man, but that you wish to enter the service of a merchant. Has hardship befallen you, Brahmin, to make you seek such a post?"

"No," Siddhartha said, "hardship has not befallen me. Indeed, I have never suffered hardship. Know that I have come to you from the Samanas, among whom I lived for a long time."

"If you come from the Samanas, how could you not be suffering hardship? Are not the Samanas utterly without possessions?"

"Possessions I have none," Siddhartha said, "if this is what you mean. Certainly I have no possessions. But I lack possessions of my own free will, so this is not a hardship."

"But what will you live on if you have nothing?"

"Never before, sir, have I occupied myself with this question. I have been without possessions for a good three years now and never found myself wondering what to live on."

"Then you lived off the possessions of others."

"No doubt this is so. A merchant too lives off the wealth of others."

"Well put. But he does not take from others without giving in return; he gives his goods in exchange."

"This would indeed appear to be true. Each person gives; each person takes. Such is life."

"But with your permission: If you have no possessions, what can you give?"

"Each person gives what he has. The warrior gives strength, the merchant gives his goods, the teacher his doctrine, the farmer rice, the fisherman fish."

"Most certainly. And so what is it you have to give? What have you learned? What are your abilities?"

"I can think. I can wait. I can fast."

"Is that all?"

"I believe it is."

"And what use are these things? Fasting, for instance— what purpose does it serve?"

"It is most excellent, sir. If a person has nothing to eat, then fasting is the most sensible thing he can do. If, for example, Siddhartha had not learned to fast, he would be compelled to take up some service or other straightaway, be it with you or wherever else, for his hunger would force him to do so. But Siddhartha can wait calmly. He knows no impatience, no urgent hardship; hunger can besiege him for a long time and just make him laugh. This, sir, is the usefulness of fasting."

"You are right, Samana. Wait for a moment."

Kamaswami went out and returned with a scroll, which he handed to his guest. "Can you read this?"

Siddhartha looked at the scroll, on which a bill of sale was written, and began to read its contents aloud.

"Splendid," Kamaswami said. "And would you mind writing something on this paper for me?"

He gave him paper and a stylus, and Siddhartha wrote and gave the paper back to him. Kamaswami read: *"Writing is good, thinking is better. Cleverness is good, patience is better."*

"You write admirably," the merchant said in praise. "We still have many things to discuss together. For today I would ask that you be my guest and take up residence in my home."

Siddhartha thanked him and accepted, and now he was living in the home of the tradesman. Clothing was brought to him, and shoes, and a servant prepared a bath for him daily. Twice a day an opulent meal was served, but Siddhartha ate only once a day, and he neither ate meat nor drank wine. Kamaswami told him of his trading, showed him goods and storerooms, showed him his accounts, and Siddhartha learned many new things. He listened much and spoke little and, mindful of Kamala's words, he never behaved subserviently toward the merchant. Instead, he compelled him to treat him as an equal: indeed, as more than an equal. Kamaswami pursued his business with solicitousness, even with passion, but Siddhartha saw it all as a game whose rules he was striving to learn but whose substance did not touch his heart.

Not long after arriving in Kamaswami's house, Siddhartha began to take part in his business dealings. Daily, however, at the hour chosen by her, he visited beautiful Kamala dressed in attractive clothes and fine shoes, and soon he was also bringing her presents. Her clever red mouth taught him many things. Her delicate, nimble hand taught him many things. He—who in matters of love was still a boy and tended to hurl himself blindly and insatiably into pleasure as into an abyss—was now being instructed methodically in this doctrine: that one cannot receive pleasure without giving pleasure; that every gesture, every caress, every touch, every glance, every inch of the body had its secret; and that awakening this secret brought happiness to the one who held this knowledge. She taught him that lovers may not part after celebrating their love until each has admired the other, each been as much victor as vanquished, so that neither might be beset by surfeit or tedium or an uneasy sense of having taken advantage or been taken advantage of. He passed glorious hours in the company of this beautiful, intelligent artist; he became her pupil, her lover, her friend. The value and meaning of the life he now was leading lay here with Kamala, not in the business dealings of Kamaswami.

The merchant entrusted him with the composition of important letters and contracts and gradually became accustomed to discussing all matters of importance with him. He soon saw that while Siddhartha knew little about rice and wool, shipping and trade, he had good instincts and surpassed him, the merchant, in coolheadedness and composure, in the art of listening to and sounding out other people. "This Brahmin," he said to a friend, "is not a proper merchant and will never be one; never is his heart passionately engaged in our transactions. But he has the secret of those to whom success comes of its own accord, be it that he was born under a lucky star, be it magic, be it something he learned among the Samanas. He seems only to be playing at doing business. Never do the transactions have any real effect on him; never are they his master; never does he fear failure or worry over a loss."

The friend advised the tradesman, "Give him a third of the profits in the transactions he arranges for you, but let him also bear the same share of the losses when there is a loss. This will make him more assiduous."

Kamaswami took this advice. Siddhartha, however, seemed not to take much notice. When there was a profit, he accepted his third with composure; when there was a loss, he laughed and said, "Oh, look, this time it went badly!"

It really did seem as if these business matters were of no interest to him. Once he traveled to a village to purchase a large rice harvest, but when he arrived the rice had already been sold to another tradesman. Nevertheless, Siddhartha remained in this village for several days; he arranged a feast for the peasants, distributed copper coins among their children, helped celebrate a marriage, and returned from his trip in the best of spirits.

Kamaswami reproached him for not having returned home at once, saying he had wasted money and time.

Siddhartha answered, "Do not scold me, dear friend! Never has anything been achieved by scolding. If there are losses, let me bear them. I am very pleased with this journey. I made the acquaintance of many different people, a Brahmin befriended me, children rode on my knees, peasants showed me their fields, and no one took me for a tradesman."

"How very lovely!" Kamaswami cried out indignantly. "But in fact a tradesman is just what you are! Or did you undertake this journey solely for your own pleasure?"

"Certainly." Siddhartha laughed. "Certainly I undertook the journey for my pleasure. Why else? I got to know new people and regions, enjoyed kindness and trust, found friendship. You see, dear friend, had I been Kamaswami, I'd have hurried home in bad spirits the moment I saw my purchase foiled, and indeed money and time would have been lost. But by staying on as I did, I had some agreeable days, learned things, and enjoyed pleasures, harming neither myself nor others with haste and bad spirits. And if ever I should return to this place, perhaps to buy some future harvest or for whatever other purpose, I shall be greeted happily and in friendship by friendly people and I shall praise myself for not having displayed haste and displeasure on my first visit. So be content, friend, and do not harm yourself by scolding! When the day arrives when you see that this Siddhartha is bringing you harm, just say the word and Siddhartha will be on his way. But until that day, let us be satisfied with each other."

In vain did the merchant attempt to convince Siddhartha that he was, after all, eating his, Kamaswami's, bread. Siddhartha ate his own bread, or rather both of them ate the bread of others, communal bread. Never did Siddhartha have a willing ear for Kamaswami's worries, and Kamaswami's worries were many. If a transaction in progress appeared threatened with failure, if a shipment of goods seemed to have gone astray, or if a debtor appeared unable to repay his debt, Kamaswami was never able to persuade Siddhartha that it was useful to speak words of worry or of anger, to have a wrinkled brow, or to sleep poorly. When Kamaswami once reproached him, saying he had, after all, learned everything he knew from him, Siddhartha replied, "Please don't make such jokes at my expense! From you I learned how much a basket of fish costs, and how much interest one can charge for borrowed money. These are your spheres of knowledge. I did not learn how to think from you, most esteemed Kamaswami; it would be better if you tried learning this from me!"

In fact, his heart wasn't in his trading. Conducting business was good because it brought him money for Kamala—indeed, much more than he needed. As for the rest, Siddhartha's interest and curiosity were piqued only by those whose trades, crafts, worries, amusements, and follies had once been as foreign and distant to him as the moon. Easy as it was for him to converse with everyone, live with everyone, learn from everyone, he was nonetheless quite aware that there was something separating him from them, and this thing that set him apart was his life as a Samana. He observed people living in a childish or animal way that he simultaneously loved and deplored. He saw their struggles, watched them suffer and turn gray over things that seemed to him utterly unworthy of such a price—things like money, petty pleasures, petty honors. He saw people scold and insult one another, saw them wailing over aches and pains that would just make a Samana smile, suffering on account of deprivations a Samana would not notice.

He was open to everything these people brought him. He welcomed the tradesman with canvas for sale, welcomed the debtor seeking a loan, welcomed the beggar who reeled off the hour-long saga of his poverty and yet was not half so poor as any Samana. The wealthy foreign merchant received the same treatment from him as the servant who shaved him and the street peddler whom he allowed to cheat him of small change when he bought bananas. When Kamaswami came to him to bemoan his worries or reproach him on account of some business matter, he listened cheerfully and with interest, found him curious, tried to understand him, conceded one or another point, just as much as seemed necessary, then turned to greet the next person who desired his attention. And there were many who came to see him. Many came to do business, many to cheat him, many to sound him out surreptitiously, many to appeal to his pity, many to hear his advice. He dispensed advice, he pitied, he gave presents, he allowed himself to be cheated a little, and this whole game—along with the passion with which everyone else was pursuing it—occupied his thoughts just as fully as they had once been occupied by the gods and Brahman.

At times he felt, deep down in his breast, a faint, dying voice faintly warning him, faintly lamenting, so faint he could scarcely hear it. At once he would become conscious for an hour that he was living a strange life, that all the things he was doing here were but a game, and that, while he was in good spirits and at times felt joy, life itself was nonetheless rushing by without touching him. Like a juggler with his balls, he was just playing in his business dealings with the people around him, watching them, taking his pleasure in them; his heart, the fountainhead of his being, was not in it. This fountainhead was flowing somewhere else, as if far distant from him, invisibly flowing and flowing, no longer part of his life. Now and again he was seized with horror at these thoughts and wished that he too might be permitted to join in all these childish goings-on with passion, with all his heart—that he might be permitted truly to live, truly to act, truly to enjoy and live rather than just standing there as a spectator.

But again and again he returned to beautiful Kamala, learned the art of love, practiced the cult of pleasure in which, more than in any other sphere, giving and taking become one. He conversed with her, learned from her, gave her counsel, received counsel. She understood him better than Govinda had once understood him; she resembled him more closely.

Once he said to her, "You are like me; you are different from most people. You are Kamala, nothing else, and within you there is a stillness and a refuge into which you can withdraw at any moment and be at home within yourself, just as I can. Few people have this, and yet all people could have it."

"Not all people are clever," Kamala said.

"No," Siddhartha said, "that isn't the reason. Kamaswami is just as clever as I am, but he has no refuge within himself. And there are people who have one whose minds are like those of little children. Most people, Kamala, are like a falling leaf as it twists and turns its way through the air, lurches and tumbles to the ground. Others, though—a very few—are like stars set on a fixed course; no wind can reach them, and they carry their law and their path within them. Among all the many learned men and Samanas I have known, there was just one who was like this, a perfect man. Never will I forget him: Gautama, the Sublime One, who preached this doctrine. Thousands of disciples hear his doctrine every day and do as he instructs, but all of them are just falling leaves. Within themselves they have no doctrine and no law."

Kamala looked at him with a smile. "Again you are speaking of him," she said. "Again you are having Samana thoughts."

Siddhartha fell silent, and they played a game of love, one of the thirty or forty different games Kamala knew. Her body was lithe, like that of a jaguar and like a hunter's bow; he who had learned love from her was adept at many pleasures, many secrets. For a long time she played with Siddhartha, coaxing him, pushing him away, forcing him, clasping him to her, taking pleasure in his mastery, until he was vanquished and lay exhausted at her side.

The hetaera bent over him, gazing long into his face, into his weary eyes.

"In the art of love," she said thoughtfully, "you are the best I've ever seen. You are stronger than others, more agile, more willing. Well have you learned my art, Siddhartha. Some day, when I am older, I wish to bear your child. And yet all this time, beloved, you have remained a Samana. Even now you do not love me; you love no one. Is it not so?"

"It may be so," Siddhartha said wearily. "I am like you. You, too, do not love—how else could you practice love as an art? Perhaps people of our sort are incapable of love. The child people can love; that is their secret."

SANSARA

For a long time Siddhartha had been living the worldly life with its pleasures but was not part of it. His senses, which he had suffocated during parched years of Samana existence, had once more awoken—he had tasted great riches, voluptuousness, power—yet in his heart he had remained a Samana for a long time. Kamala, that clever woman, had been right about this. Always the arts of thinking, waiting, and fasting had guided him in his life, and those who lived a worldly existence—the child people—had remained foreign to him, as he was to them.

The years flew by, and Siddhartha, swaddled in well-being, scarcely felt their passing. He had grown rich, he had long since acquired a house of his own, servants of his own, and a garden beside the river outside of town. People liked him, they came to him when they needed money or counsel, but no one was close to him except Kamala.

That noble, bright awakening he had experienced once, at the height of his youth, in the days following Gautama's sermon, after his parting from Govinda—that eager expectancy, that proud standing alone without teachers or doctrines, that supple readiness to hear the divine voice within his own heart—had gradually faded into memory; it had been transitory. Distant and faint was the sound of the holy fountainhead that had once been near, that had once murmured inside him. To be sure, much of what he had learned—from the Samanas, from Gautama, from his father the Brahmin—had remained with him for a long time: moderate living, enjoyment of thought, hours devoted to *samadhi,* secret knowledge of the Self, that eternal being that is neither body nor consciousness. Much of this had remained with him, but one thing after another had settled to the bottom and been covered with dust. Just as a potter's wheel, once set in motion, will continue to spin for a long time, only slowly wearying and coming to rest, so had the wheel of asceticism, the wheel of thought, and the wheel of differentiation gone on spinning for a long time in Siddhartha's soul, and they were spinning still, but this spin was growing slow and hesitant; it was coming to a standstill. Slowly, as moisture seeps into the dying tree trunk, slowly filling it up and making it rot, worldliness and lethargy had crept into Siddhartha's soul, filling it slowly, making it heavy, making it weary, putting it to sleep. At the same time, however, his senses had come to life; they had learned many things, experienced many things.

Siddhartha had learned to conduct business, to wield power over people, to take pleasure with a woman; he had learned to wear nice clothes, give orders to servants, and bathe in sweet-smelling water. He had learned to eat dishes prepared with delicacy and care, even fish, even flesh and fowl, spices and sweets, and to drink wine, which brings lethargy and forgetfulness. He had learned to throw dice and play chess, to be entertained by dancing girls, have himself carried about in a sedan chair, sleep in a soft bed. But still he had felt himself to be different from the others, superior to them, still he had watched them with a certain disdain, a certain contempt, that very contempt a Samana always feels for the worldly. When Kamaswami was indisposed, when he was cross, when he felt slighted, when he was tortured by his mercantile woes, Siddhartha had always observed this disdainfully. Only slowly and imperceptibly, with the coming and going of the harvests and monsoons, had his disdain grown weary, his superiority waned. Only slowly, among his growing riches, had Siddhartha himself taken on some of the characteristics of the child people, something of their childlike manner and fearfulness. And yet he envied them, envying them more the more he came to resemble them. He envied them the one thing they possessed that he was lacking: the importance they were capable of attaching to their lives, their passionate joys and fears, the happiness, uneasy but sweet, of their eternal infatuations. For infatuated they were—with themselves, with women, with their children, with honor or money, with plans or hopes. But this childish joy and childish folly he had not learned from them, this one thing remained unlearned; all he was learning from them were unpleasant things that he himself despised. It happened more and more often now that he remained lying in bed for a long time the day after an evening of conviviality, feeling stupid and weary. It would happen that he became cross and impatient when Kamaswami bored him with his worries. It would happen that he laughed too loudly when he lost at dice. His face was still more clever and spiritual than others, but it seldom smiled, and one after the other it was taking on the traits one so often observes in the faces of the wealthy: that look of dissatisfaction, infirmity, displeasure, lethargy, unkindness. Slowly he was being stricken with the maladies that afflict rich people's souls.

Like a veil or a thin fog, weariness descended upon Siddhartha, slowly, a bit thicker each day, a bit hazier each month, a bit heavier each year. Just as a new garment gets old with time, loses its attractive colors, becomes stained, wrinkled, and worn at the seams, and here and there begins to display unfortunate threadbare patches, so too had the new life that Siddhartha began after parting from Govinda gotten old and with the passing of the years begun to lose its color and sheen; wrinkles and stains were collecting on it, and—hidden beneath the surface but already peeking out hideously now and again—disillusionment and nausea lay waiting. This Siddhartha did not notice. He noticed only that the bright and certain inner voice that once had awoken within him and accompanied him unceasingly in his days of glory had fallen silent.

The world had captured him: voluptuousness, lust, lethargy, and in the end even greed, the vice he'd always thought the most foolish and had despised and scorned above all others. Property, ownership, and riches had captured him in the end. No longer were they just games to him, trifles; they had become chains and burdens. A curious and slippery path had led Siddhartha to his latest and vilest form of dependency: dice playing. Ever since he had ceased to be a Samana in his heart, Siddhartha had begun to pursue these games with their stakes of money and precious goods—games he had once participated in offhandedly, dismissing them as a child-people custom—with growing frenzy and passion. He was feared as a player. Few dared to challenge him, for his bets were fierce and reckless. He played this game out of his heart's distress. Losing and squandering the wretched money was an angry pleasure; in no other way could he have shown his contempt for wealth, the idol of the merchants, more clearly and with more pronounced scorn. And so he bet high and mercilessly. Despising himself, mocking himself, he won thousands and threw thousands away, gambled away money, gambled away jewelry, gambled away a country house, won again, lost again. That fear—that terrible and oppressive fear he felt while rolling the dice, while worrying over his own high stakes—he loved it. Again and again he sought to renew it, to increase it, to goad it to a higher level of intensity, for only in the grasp of this fear did he still feel something like happiness, something like intoxication, something like exalted life in the midst of his jaded, dull, insipid existence. And after each major loss he dreamed of new wealth, pursued his trading with increased vigor, and put more pressure on his debtors, for he wanted to go on gambling, he wanted to go on squandering all he could so as to continue to show his contempt for wealth. Siddhartha lost the composure with which he had once greeted losses, he lost his patience when others were tardy with their payments, lost his good-naturedness when beggars came to call, lost all desire to give gifts and loan money to supplicants. The one who laughed as he gambled away ten thousand on a single toss of the dice turned intolerant and petty in his business dealings, and at night he sometimes dreamed of money. Whenever he awoke from this hateful spell, whenever he saw his face grown older and uglier in the mirror on his bedroom wall, whenever he was assailed by shame and nausea, he fled further, seeking to escape in more gambling, seeking to numb himself with sensuality and wine, and then hurled himself back into the grind of hoarding and acquisition. In this senseless cycle he ran himself ragged, ran himself old, ran himself sick.

Then one day a dream came to warn him. He had spent the evening hours with Kamala in her beautiful pleasure garden. They had sat beneath the trees, deep in conversation, and Kamala had spoken sober words, words behind which grief and weariness lay hidden. She had asked him to tell her about Gautama and couldn't get enough of hearing how pure his eyes were, how still and beautiful his mouth, how kind his smile, how peaceful his gait. Having made him go on telling stories of the sublime Buddha for a long time, Kamala had sighed and said, "One day, perhaps soon, I too will follow this

Buddha. I will give him my pleasure garden and take refuge in his doctrine." But then she aroused him and bound him to her in love play with an anguished passion, biting him and wetting him with tears, as if trying to squeeze the last sweet drop from this vain, transitory pleasure. Never before had it seemed so strangely clear to Siddhartha how closely sensuality was linked to death. He had lain at Kamala's side with her face close beside his, and beneath her eyes and beside the corners of her mouth he was able to read clearly as never before an anxious script, a writing made of tiny lines, quiet furrows, writing that called to mind autumn and age, just as Siddhartha himself, who was only in his forties, had already noticed gray hairs here and there among the black. Weariness was inscribed in Kamala's beautiful face, weariness from walking a long path that had no happy goal, weariness and the first signs of withering, and a secret anxiety, not yet uttered, perhaps not yet even recognized: fear of old age, fear of autumn, fear of having to die. Sighing, he had taken leave of her, his soul full of reluctance and secret apprehension.

Siddhartha had spent the night in his home with dancing girls and wine, had made a show of superiority before others of his standing, though he was no longer superior, had drunk a great deal of wine, and had gone to bed long after midnight, weary and yet agitated, close to tears and despair. For a long time he sought sleep in vain, his heart full of a misery he felt he could no longer endure, full of a nausea that coursed through him like the vile, insipid taste of the wine, like the dreary all-too-sweet music, the all-too-soft smiles of the dancers, the all-too-sweet perfume of their hair and breasts. But nothing made the nausea well up in him more bitterly than did he himself: He felt nausea at his perfumed hair, the smell of wine on his breath, the weary slackness and reluctance of his skin. Just as someone who has eaten or drunk too much vomits it up again in agony and yet is glad for the relief, sleepless Siddhartha yearned for a monstrous wave of nausea that would rid him of these pleasures, these habits, this whole meaningless existence and himself along with it. Only with the first rays of morning and with the first stirrings in the street outside his town house had he sunk into slumber and found a few moments of half numbness, a suggestion of sleep. During these moments he had a dream.

Kamala kept a rare little songbird in a golden cage; he dreamed about this bird. He dreamed the bird, which always used to sing at dawn, had fallen silent, and since the silence struck him, he went over to the cage and looked inside; the little bird lay dead and still on the bottom. He took it out, weighed it for a moment in his hand, and then tossed it aside, into the street, and at the same moment he was seized with fear and horror and his heart hurt, as if with this dead bird he had thrust aside everything that had worth and value.

Waking from this dream with a start, he felt himself surrounded by deep sadness. Devoid of value, it seemed to him, devoid of value and meaning was this life he'd been living; nothing that was alive, nothing in any way precious or worthy of keeping, had remained in his hands. Alone he stood, and empty, like a shipwrecked man upon the shore.

His mood black, Siddhartha betook himself to a pleasure garden that belonged to him, locked the gate, and sat down beneath a mango tree, feeling death in his heart and horror in his breast; sitting there, he felt himself dying inside, withering inside, coming to an end. Eventually he collected his thoughts and in his mind retraced his steps along the entire path of his life, from the first days he could remember. Had he ever experienced happiness, felt true bliss? Oh, yes, he had, several times. He had tasted happiness in the years of his boyhood, when he had succeeded in winning the praise of the Brahmins by excelling, far beyond all others of his age, at reciting the holy verses, debating with the learned men, and assisting at the sacrifices. He had felt then, in his heart, "A path lies before you to which you are called; the gods are waiting for you." And again as a young man, when he had been whisked from the horde of his peers and swept aloft in pursuit of the ever-ascending goal of all thought, when he was struggling painfully to grasp the meaning of Brahman, when every shred of knowledge he attained only gave rise to new thirst within him—then too he had felt it, amid all the thirst, amid all the pain: "Strive on! Strive on! You have a calling!" He had heard this voice when he left home and chose the life of a Samana, he had heard it again when he left the Samanas to seek out the Perfect One, and again when he had left Gautama to venture into the Unknown. How long had it been since he had last heard that voice, how long since he had ascended to new heights. How tedious and flat was the path he had been following these many long years, with no lofty goal, no thirst, no exaltation, years of contenting himself with small pleasures and yet never being satisfied! For all these years he had been longing and attempting, without being aware of it, to become like these many people, these children, and all the while his life had been far more miserable and impoverished than theirs, for their goals were not his, nor their worries; this entire world of Kamaswami people had been a mere game to him, a dance he was observing, a comedy. Only Kamala had been dear to him, only she was of value—but was she still? Did he still need her, or she him? Were they not playing a game that had no end? Was it necessary to live for *that*? No, it was not necessary! This game was called Sansara, a game for children, a game to be played sweetly perhaps, once, twice, ten times—but again and again?

Siddhartha realized that the game was over; he could no longer play it. A shudder coursed through his body; within him, he felt, something had died.

That entire day he sat beneath the mango tree thinking of

his father, thinking of Govinda, thinking of Gautama. Had he had to leave them all behind to become a Kamaswami? He was still sitting there when night arrived. Glancing up and seeing the stars, he thought, Here I am sitting beneath my mango tree in my pleasure garden. He smiled a little—was it necessary, was it fitting, was it not rather a foolish game that he owned a mango tree, that he owned a garden?

This too he now brought to a close; this too died within him. He stood up, took leave of the mango tree, took leave of the pleasure garden. As he had eaten no food that day, he felt intense hunger and thought of his house in town, his bedchamber and bed, the table covered with food. With a weary smile, he shook himself and took leave of these things.

The very same hour that night, Siddhartha left his garden, left the city, and never returned. It was a long time before Kamaswami stopped sending out servants to look for him, for he believed Siddhartha had fallen into the hands of robbers. Kamala sent no one. When she learned that Siddhartha had vanished, she felt no surprise. Had she not always been expecting this? Was he not a Samana, a pilgrim, bound to no home? She had felt this more strongly than ever the last time they had been together, and despite the pain of her loss she felt glad that she had pressed him to her breast with such ardor that last time, that she had felt, one last time, so utterly possessed by him, permeated by him.

When she first received word of Siddhartha's disappearance, she went to the window, where she had been keeping a rare songbird imprisoned in a golden cage. She opened the door of the cage, took the bird out, and let it fly away. For a long time she gazed after it, the flying bird. From that day on she received no more visitors and kept her house closed. Soon afterward it became apparent that her last encounter with Siddhartha had left her pregnant.

BESIDE THE RIVER

Siddhartha wandered through the forest, already quite far from the city, knowing only this: He could never go back again. The life he had been living these many years was now over and done with; he had drunk it to the lees, sucked the last drops, filled himself with nausea. Dead was the songbird from his dream. Dead was the bird within his heart. He was deeply enmeshed in Sansara, had absorbed nausea and death from all sides the way a sponge soaks up water till it is full. He was filled with antipathy, filled with misery, filled with death; there was nothing left in the world that could tempt him, console him, give him pleasure.

He longed to be rid of himself, to find peace, to be dead. If only a bolt of lightning would strike him down! If only a tiger would devour him! If only there were a wine, a poison, that would numb him, bring him oblivion and sleep, and no more awakenings! Was there any sort of filth with which he had not yet defiled himself, any sin or folly he had not committed, any barrenness of soul he had not brought upon himself? Was it still possible to live? Was it possible to continue, over and over again, to draw breath, to exhale, to feel hunger, to eat again, to sleep again, to lie again beside a woman? Had not this cycle been exhausted for him, concluded?

Siddhartha came to the great river that ran through the forest, the same river across which a ferryman had once transported him in the days of his youth, when he was just leaving Gautama's town. Beside this river he now stopped and remained standing hesitantly upon its bank. Weariness and hunger had made him weak. What reason did he have to continue walking—walking where, and with what goal? No, there were no more goals; all that was left was a deep painful longing to shake off this whole mad dream, to spit out this stale wine, to put an end to this pitiful, shameful existence.

Above the riverbank, a tree grew aslant, a coconut palm, and against its trunk Siddhartha rested his shoulder, placing his arm around the tree and gazing down into the green water that flowed on and on beneath him, gazed down and found himself utterly overwhelmed by the desire to let go and sink beneath its surface. A terrible emptiness was reflected back at him from beneath the water, which found its reply in the awful emptiness within his soul. He had reached an impasse. All that was left for him to do was annihilate himself, smash to pieces the botched structure of his life, throw it away, hurl it at the feet of the mocking gods. This was the great purging he had longed for: death, the smashing of the form he so despised! Let the fish devour him, this dog Siddhartha, this madman, this spoiled and rotten body, this sagging and abused soul! Let the fish and the crocodiles devour him, let demons tear him to pieces!

With a grimace, he peered into the water, saw his face mirrored there, and spit at it. Feeling profound weariness, he released his arm from around the tree trunk and rotated his body a little so as to let himself fall vertically, sink at last into the depths. With closed eyes, he sank toward death.

Then, from distant reaches of his soul, from bygone realms

of his weary life, a sound fluttered. It was a word, a syllable that he now spoke aloud, mindlessly, his voice a babble, the first and final word of every Brahmin prayer, the holy *Om* that meant *the perfect* or *perfection*. And the moment the sound *Om* touched Siddhartha's ear, his slumbering spirit suddenly awoke and recognized the foolishness of his actions.

Siddhartha was deeply shaken. This, then, was how things stood with him. He was so lost, so befuddled and bereft of knowledge as to have been capable of wanting to die, of letting this wish, this childish wish, grow large inside him: the wish to find peace by annihilating his body! All the torments of the last months, all the disillusionment, all the despair had been unable to achieve this thing that had been accomplished in the single moment when the *Om* pierced his consciousness: his recognizing himself in his misery and folly.

"*Om*," he said aloud. "*Om!*" And he had knowledge of Brahman, had knowledge of the indestructibility of life, had knowledge of all things divine that he had forgotten.

But all this was only a moment, a flash. Siddhartha sank down at the foot of the coconut palm, laid his head upon the root of the tree, and fell into a deep slumber.

Deep was his sleep and free of dreams; it had been a long time since he had known such sleep. When he awoke some hours later, it seemed to him as if ten years had passed. He heard the water quietly flowing, didn't know where he was or who had brought him, opened his eyes, was astonished to see trees and sky above him—and then remembered where he was and how he had come here. But it took him quite a while to do this, and the past appeared to him as if concealed behind a veil, infinitely distant, infinitely removed from him, infinitely indifferent. He knew only that his former life—in his first moment of new awareness, this former life appeared to him like a previous incarnation from the distant past, an early embodiment of his present Self—his former life had been left behind, that he had even wanted to throw away his life in his nausea and misery, but that he had regained consciousness beneath a coconut palm with the holy word *Om* upon his lips; he had then fallen asleep, and now, having awoken, he beheld the world as a new man. Murmuring to himself the word *Om,* over which he had fallen asleep, he felt as if this entire sleep had been nothing but a long deeply engrossed chanting of *Om,* an *Om*-thinking, a plunging into and complete immersion in *Om,* in the Nameless, the Perfect.

What a wonderful sleep it had been! Never had a sleep so refreshed him, so renewed him, so rejuvenated him! Could it be that he had really died, perished, and been reborn in a new shape? But no, he recognized himself, recognized his hand and his feet, recognized the place where he lay, recognized this ego within his breast, this obstinate, strange creature Siddhartha; but this Siddhartha was nonetheless transformed, was renewed, was oddly well rested, oddly awake, joyful, and filled with curiosity.

When Siddhartha sat up, he saw a man seated across from him, a stranger, a monk dressed in a yellow robe with a shaved head, sitting in the pose used for contemplation. He regarded this man, who had neither hair on his head nor a beard, and he had not looked at him for long before he recognized this monk as Govinda, the friend of his youth, Govinda who had taken his refuge with the sublime Buddha. Govinda too had aged, but still his face displayed the same features as before: They spoke of eagerness, of fidelity, of searching, of apprehension. But when Govinda, feeling his gaze, raised his eyes to look at him, Siddhartha saw that Govinda did not recognize him. Govinda was pleased to find him awake; apparently he had been sitting here a long time waiting for him to awaken although he did not know him.

"I was asleep," Siddhartha said. "How did you get here?"

"You were asleep," Govinda replied. "It is not good to sleep in such places where there are often snakes and the creatures of the forest have their paths. I, master, am a disciple of the sublime Gautama, the Buddha, the Sakyamuni, and was on a pilgrimage along this path with others of our order when I saw you lying asleep in a place where it is dangerous to sleep. For this reason I attempted to rouse you, master, and when I saw that your sleep was very sound, I remained behind to sit with you. And then, it appears, I myself fell asleep—I who had intended to watch over you. I have performed my duties poorly; weariness overcame me. But now that you are awake, let me go, that I might catch up with my brothers."

"I thank you, Samana, for guarding my sleep," Siddhartha said. "You disciples of the Sublime One are most kind. Now you may go."

"I will go, master. May you always find yourself well."

"I thank you, Samana."

Govinda made the gesture of leave-taking and said, "Farewell."

"Farewell, Govinda," said Siddhartha.

The monk stopped short.

"Forgive me, master. How do you know my name?"

Siddhartha smiled. "I know you, Govinda, from your father's hut, and from the Brahmin school, and from the sacrifices, and from our journey to the Samanas, and from that hour in the grove of Jetavana when you took your refuge with the Sublime One."

"You are Siddhartha!" Govinda cried out. "Now I recognize you; I cannot understand how I could have failed to recognize you before. Welcome, Siddhartha. Great is my joy at seeing you once more."

"I too am joyful at seeing you. You were the guardian of my sleep; again I thank you for this, although I was in no need of a guardian. Where are you going, my friend?"

"I am going nowhere. We monks are always journeying so

long as it is not monsoon season; constantly we travel from one place to another, living according to the rules; we preach the doctrine, accept alms, and go on. Always it is so. But you, Siddhartha, where are you going?"

Siddhartha said, "It is just the same with me as with you, my friend. I am going nowhere. I am merely journeying, I am on a pilgrimage."

Govinda said, "You say you are a pilgrim, and I believe you. But forgive me, Siddhartha; a pilgrim does not look as you do. You wear the clothes of a rich man, you wear the shoes of an elegant gentleman, and your hair smells of scented water; it is not the hair of a pilgrim, not the hair of a Samana."

"Indeed, dear friend, you have observed all this well; your keen eye misses nothing. But I did not say to you that I was a Samana. I said I am on a pilgrimage—and, indeed, I am a pilgrim."

"You are a pilgrim," Govinda said. "But few men embark on pilgrimages wearing such clothes, with such shoes, with such hair. Never, in all my years of pilgrimage, have I encountered such a pilgrim as you."

"I believe you, my Govinda. But now, today, you *have* met just such a pilgrim, in such shoes, with such garments. Remember, my friend: The world of shapes is transitory, and transitory—highly transitory—are our clothes, the way we wear our hair, and our hair and bodies themselves. I wear the garments of a rich man; you discerned this quite correctly. I wear them because I *was* rich, and I wear my hair like one of the worldly creatures, the lechers, for I was one of them."

"And now, Siddhartha, what are you now?"

"This I do not know. I have as little an idea as you do. I am on a journey. I was a rich man and am rich no longer, and what I will be tomorrow I do not know."

"You have lost your riches?"

"I have lost them, or they have lost me. They are no longer mine. Swiftly does the wheel of shapes turn, Govinda. Where is the Brahmin Siddhartha? Where is the Samana Siddhartha? Where is the rich man Siddhartha? The transitory changes swiftly, Govinda, as you know."

Govinda gazed at the friend of his youth for a long time, his eyes full of doubt. Then he took leave of him in the way one takes leave of a distinguished gentleman and went on his way.

With a smiling face, Siddhartha watched him walk off; he still loved him, this faithful friend, this apprehensive one. How, at this moment, in this glorious hour after his wonderful sleep, suffused with *Om*, could he have failed to love anyone or anything? This was precisely the form of the enchantment that the *Om* had wrought within him as he slept: He loved everything and was filled with joyous love for all he saw, and he realized that what had so ailed him before was that he had been able to love nothing and no one.

With a smiling face, Siddhartha gazed after the departing monk. His sleep had restored him, but he was still tormented by hunger, for he had eaten nothing for two days and the time when he had been impervious to hunger was now long past. With sorrow, yet also with laughter, he thought of this time. Back then, he recalled, he had boasted of three things before Kamala, the three noble and unassailable arts he had mastered: fasting—waiting—thinking. These had been his possessions, his power and strength, his sturdy staff; it was these three arts he had studied in the assiduous, laborious years of his youth, to the exclusion of all else. And now they had abandoned him; not one of them remained, not fasting, not waiting, not thinking. He had sacrificed them for the most miserable of things, the most transitory: for sensual pleasure, for luxury, for wealth! How strangely things had gone with him. And now, it appeared, he had truly become one of the child people.

Siddhartha considered his circumstances. Thinking did not come easily to him. He didn't really feel like it, but he forced himself.

Now that all these utterly transitory things have slipped away from me, he thought, I am left under the sun just as I stood here once as a small child; I own nothing, know nothing, can do nothing, have learned nothing. How curious this is! Now that I am no longer young, now that my hair is already half gray and my strength is beginning to wane, I am starting over again from the beginning, from childhood! Again he had to smile. Yes, it certainly was strange, this fate of his! Things were going downhill with him, and now he was once more standing in the world, empty and naked and foolish. But he could not quite bring himself to feel sorrowful on this account. Indeed, he felt a tremendous urge to burst out laughing: laughter at himself, laughter at this strange, foolish world.

Things are going downhill with you! he said to himself, laughing, and as he said this his eyes came to rest upon the river, and he saw the river too going downhill, wandering always downhill and singing gaily all the while. This pleased him greatly, and he gave the river a friendly smile. Was this not the river in which he had wished to drown once, a hundred years before, or had it only been a dream?

Curious indeed this life of mine has been, he thought, it has taken such strange detours. As a boy I was concerned only with gods and sacrifices. As a youth I was concerned only with asceticism, with thinking and *samadhi;* I went searching for Brahman, revered the eternal in Atman. But as a young man I set off after the penitents, lived in the forest, suffered heat and frost, learned to go without food, taught my body to feel nothing. How glorious it was then when realization came to me in the doctrine of the great Buddha; I felt knowledge of the Oneness of the world coursing through me like my own blood. But even the Buddha and his great knowledge had to be left behind. I went off and learned the pleasures of love from Kamala, learned to conduct business from Kamaswami, accumulated money, squandered money, learned to love my stomach, learned to indulge my senses. I had to spend many years losing my spirit, unlearning how to think, forgetting the great Oneness. Is it not as if I were slowly and circuitously turning from a man into a child, from a thinker into one of the child people? And still this path has been very good, and still the bird in my breast has not died. But what a path it has been! I have had to pass through so much foolishness, so much vice, so much error, so much nausea and disillusionment and wretchedness, merely in order to become a child again and be able to start over. But all of this was just and proper; my heart is saying yes, and my eyes are laughing. I had to experience despair, I had to sink to the most foolish of all thoughts, the thought of suicide, to be able to experience grace, to hear *Om* again, to be able to sleep well and awaken well. I had to become a fool to find Atman within me once more. I had to sin to be able to live again. Where else may my path be taking me? How stupid it is, this path of mine; it goes in loops. For all I know it's going in a circle. Let it lead where it will, I shall follow it.

He felt joy welling up gloriously within his breast.

Tell me, he asked his heart, what is the source of all this gladness? Might it come from this long, good slumber that has so restored me? Or from the word *Om* that I uttered? Or because I have escaped, because my flight was successful, because I am finally free again and standing like a child beneath the sky? Oh, how good it is to have fled, to have become free! How pure and beautiful the air is here, how good it is to breathe it! In the place I ran from, everything smelled of lotions, of spices, of wine, of excess, of lethargy. How I hated the world of rich men, of gluttons, of gamblers! How I hated myself for having remained so long in that hideous world!

How I hated myself; how I robbed myself, poisoned and tormented myself; how I made myself old and wicked! No, never again will I imagine, as I once enjoyed doing, that Siddhartha was a wise man! But one thing I did do well, one thing pleases me, which I must praise: All my self-hatred has now come to an end, along with that idiotic, desolate existence! I praise you, Siddhartha. After all these years of idiocy, you for once had a good idea; you did something; you heard the bird singing in your breast and followed it!

In this way he praised himself and felt pleased with himself, listening with curiosity to his stomach, which was rumbling with hunger. He had tasted his share of sorrow and misery these past days and times, tasted them and spit them out, eaten of them till he had reached the point of despair, of death. All was well. He might have remained a great while longer at Kamaswami's side, earning money, squandering money, stuffing his belly and letting his soul thirst; he might have gone on living a great while longer in this cozy well-upholstered hell if that moment had not come: that moment of utter despondency and despair, that extreme moment when he was hanging above the flowing water, ready to destroy himself. That he had felt this despair, this deepest nausea, and yet had not succumbed to it, that the bird, the happy fountainhead and voice within him, had remained alive after all—it was because of all these things that he now felt such joy, that he laughed, that his face was beaming beneath his gray hair.

It is good, he thought, to taste for oneself all that it is necessary to know. Already as a child I learned that worldly desires and wealth were not good things. I have known this for a long time but have only now experienced it. And now I do know it, know it not only with my memory but with my eyes, with my heart, and with my stomach. How glad I am to know it!

For a long time he contemplated his transformation, listening as the bird sang with joy. Had this bird not died within him, had he not felt its death? No, something else had died within him, something that had desired death for a long time. Was it not the very thing that he had once, in his ardent years as a penitent, wanted to kill? Was it not his Self, his nervous, proud little ego that he had done battle with for so many years, that had bested him again and again, that was always back again each time he killed it off, forbidding joy and feeling fear? Was it not this that had finally met its death today, here in the forest beside this lovely river? Was it not because of this death that he was now like a child, so full of trust, so devoid of fear, so full of joy?

And now it dawned on Siddhartha why, as a Brahmin and as a penitent, he had struggled in vain to subdue this ego. A surfeit of knowledge had hindered him, too many holy verses, too many rules for the sacrifices, too much self-castigation, too much activity and striving! He had been full of pride— always the cleverest, always the most eager, always a step ahead of all the others, always the knowledgeable spiritual one, always the priest or wise man. His Self had crept into this priesthood, this pride, this spirituality, and made itself at home there, growing plump, all the while he thought he was killing it off with his fasting and penitence. Now he could see it, and he saw that the secret voice had been right: No teacher would ever have been able to deliver him. This is why he'd had to go out into the world and lose himself in pleasure and power, in women and money, why he'd had to become a tradesman, a gambler, a drinker, an avaricious creature, until the priest and the Samana within him were dead. This is why he'd had to go on enduring these hateful years, enduring the nausea, the emptiness, the senselessness of a desolate, lost existence, enduring to the end, to the point of bitter despair, until even the lecher Siddhartha, the greedy Siddhartha, could die. He *had* died, and a new Siddhartha had awoken from sleep. He too would grow old; he too would have to die someday. Siddhartha was transitory, every shape was transitory. Today, though, he was young; he was a child, the new Siddhartha, and was full of joy.

Thinking these thoughts, he listened with a smile to his stomach, listened with gratitude to a buzzing bee. Gaily he looked into the flowing river: Never had a body of water so pleased him, never had he perceived the voice and the allegory of the moving water so powerfully and beautifully. It seemed to him that the river had something special to say to him, something he did not yet know, something still awaiting him. In this river Siddhartha had wished to drown, and in it the old, weary, despairing Siddhartha did indeed drown this day. The new Siddhartha, however, felt a deep love for this flowing water and resolved not to leave it again so soon.

THE FERRYMAN

I shall remain here beside this river, Siddhartha thought; it is the river I once crossed on my way to the child people. A kind ferryman took me across; I shall go to see him. From his hut he once sent me on my path to a new life that has now grown old and died. Let the path and the life I am embarking on now have their start here as well!

Lovingly he gazed into the flowing water, into the transparent green, into the crystal lines of its mysterious patterning. He saw bright pearls rising from its depths, silent bubbles floating on its surface, the blue of the sky reproduced in it. With a thousand eyes the river gazed at him: with green eyes, white eyes, crystal eyes, sky-blue eyes. How he loved this water, how it enchanted him, how grateful he was to it! In his heart he heard the voice that was awakening once more, and it said to him, Love this water! Remain beside it! Learn from it! Oh, yes, he wanted to learn from it; he wanted to listen to it. One who understood this water and its secrets, it seemed to him, would understand many other things as well, many secrets, all secrets.

But of all the water's secrets, he saw today only a single

one—one that struck his soul. He saw that this water flowed and flowed, it was constantly flowing, and yet it was always there; it was always eternally the same and yet new at every moment! Oh, to be able to grasp this, to understand it! He did not understand it, did not grasp it; he felt only an inkling stirring within him, distant memory, divine voices.

Siddhartha got to his feet; the gnawing hunger in his midsection was becoming unbearable. Lost in thought, he wandered farther along the riverbank, walking upstream, listening to the current and to the growling hunger in his belly.

When he reached the ferry, the boat was lying ready, and the very same ferryman who had once transported the young Samana across the river was standing in the boat. Siddhartha recognized him; he too had greatly aged.

"Will you ferry me across the river?" Siddhartha asked.

The ferryman, astonished to see so elegant a gentleman alone and journeying on foot, took him into the boat and pushed off from shore.

"What a beautiful life you have chosen," the passenger said. "It must be lovely to live each day beside this water and ply your oar upon it."

Smiling, the ferryman rocked with the boat as he rowed. "It is lovely, master, as you say. But is not every life, every work, lovely?"

"That may be. But I envy you yours."

"Oh, you might quickly lose your taste for it. It is nothing for people who wear fine clothes."

Siddhartha laughed. "This is not the first time I have been scrutinized this day on account of my clothing, scrutinized with distrust. Ferryman, would you accept these clothes, which are a burden to me? For you should know that I have no money with which to pay your fare."

"The gentleman is jesting." The ferryman laughed.

"It is no jest, friend. You see, this is not the first time you have ferried me across these waters in your boat out of charity. Show me the same kindness today, and accept my clothing for your troubles."

"Does the gentleman mean to continue on without clothes?"

"Oh"—Siddhartha sighed—"what I would like best would be not to continue on at all. What I would like best, ferryman, is if you were to give me an old loincloth to wear and keep me on as your assistant, or rather your apprentice, for I would first have to learn how to handle the boat."

For a long time the ferryman gazed searchingly at the stranger.

"Now I recognize you," he said at last. "You spent the night in my hut once, a long time ago, surely it's been more than twenty years, and then I ferried you across the river and we parted from each other like good friends. Were you not a Samana? I can no longer recall your name."

"My name is Siddhartha, and I was a Samana when you saw me last."

"Then welcome, Siddhartha. My name is Vasudeva. You will, I hope, be my guest tonight as well and sleep in my hut and tell me from where you have come and why your clothes are such a burden to you."

They had reached the middle of the river, and Vasudeva leaned his weight more heavily upon the oar, pressing against the current. Peacefully he worked, his eyes fixed on the boat's tip, his arms strong. Siddhartha sat watching him. He remembered how, over twenty years ago, on that final day he'd spent as a Samana, love for this man had stirred in his heart. Gratefully he now accepted Vasudeva's offer. When they reached shore, he helped tie the boat to the stakes, and then the ferryman invited him to enter the hut and set bread and water before him. Siddhartha ate with relish, and also ate with relish of the mango fruit Vasudeva offered him.

After their meal—it was nearly twilight now—they found seats upon a tree trunk on the riverbank, and Siddhartha told the ferryman of his origins and his life, just as it had passed before his eyes today, in the hour of his despair. His story lasted deep into the night.

Vasudeva listened with great attentiveness. He took in everything as he listened, origins and childhood, all the learning, all the searching, all the joy, all the suffering. This was one of the greatest among the ferryman's virtues: He had mastered the art of listening. Although Vasudeva himself did not utter a word, it was clear to the one speaking that each of his words was being allowed to enter into his listener, who sat there quietly, openly, waiting; not a single word was disregarded or met with impatience; Vasudeva attached neither praise nor blame to what he heard but merely listened. Siddhartha felt what a joy it was to be able to confide in such a listener, to entrust his life, his searching, his sorrow, to this welcoming heart.

Near the end of Siddhartha's tale, when he began to speak of the tree beside the river and his deep fall, of the holy *Om,* and how after his slumber he had felt such love for the river, the ferryman listened twice as attentively as before, utterly and completely absorbed, his eyes closed.

Then, after Siddhartha had fallen silent and some time had passed, Vasudeva said, "It is just as I thought. The river spoke to you. To you as well it is a friend; to you as well it speaks. That is good, that is very good. Stay here with me, Siddhartha my friend. Once I had a wife, her bed lay beside mine, but she died a long time ago; for a long time I have lived alone. Now you will live with me. There is plenty of room and food enough for both of us."

"I thank you," Siddhartha said. "I thank you and accept. I thank you also for listening so well to me! Rare are those who know how to listen; never before have I met anyone who was as skilled in listening as you are. This too I shall learn from you."

"You will learn this," Vasudeva said, "but not from me. It was the river that taught me to listen, and it will teach you as well. It knows everything, the river, and one can learn anything from it. You too, after all, have already learned from the river that it is good to strive for downward motion, to sink, to seek the depths. The wealthy, elegant Siddhartha will row as others bid him; the learned Brahmin Siddhartha will become a ferryman. In this too you were instructed by the river. You will learn the rest from it as well."

Siddhartha responded after a long pause. "What is the rest, Vasudeva?"

Vasudeva got up. "It has grown late," he said. "Let us go to bed. I cannot tell you what the rest is, my friend. You will learn it; perhaps you already know it. You see, I am not a learned man. I do not know how to speak, I do not even know how to think. I know only how to listen and to be pious; these are the only things I have learned. If I could say and teach these things, perhaps I would be a wise man, but as it is I am only a ferryman, and it is my task to transport people across this river. I have ferried a great many people across it, thousands, and to all of them my river was nothing more than a hindrance in their travels. They were traveling for money and for business, to weddings and on pilgrimages, and the river was in their way; the purpose of the ferryman was to carry them past this obstacle as quickly as possible. But there were a few among these thousands, just a few of them, four or five, for whom the river ceased to be an obstacle. They heard its voice, they listened to it, and the river became holy to them as it has become holy to me. Let us retire now, Siddhartha."

Siddhartha stayed with the ferryman and learned to handle the boat, and when there was nothing to do at the ferry he worked with Vasudeva in the rice paddy, gathered wood, and picked the fruit of the pisang trees. He learned to hammer to-gether an oar and to repair the boat and to weave baskets; he was joyful over all he learned, and the days and months went swiftly past. But even more than Vasudeva could teach him, he learned from the river, which taught him unceasingly. Above all, it taught him how to listen—how to listen with a quiet heart and a waiting, open soul, without passion, without desire, without judgment, without opinion.

He lived beside Vasudeva as one friend beside another, and from time to time they exchanged words, a few carefully con-sidered words. Vasudeva was no friend of words, so Sid-dhartha rarely succeeded in moving him to speech.

"Have you too," he asked him once, "have you too learned this secret from the river: that time does not exist?"

Vasudeva's face broke into a radiant smile. "Yes, Sid-dhartha," he said. "Is this what you mean: that the river is in all places at once, at its source and where it flows into the sea, at the waterfall, at the ferry, at the rapids, in the ocean, in the mountains, everywhere at once, so for the river there is only the present moment and not the shadow of a future?"

"It is," Siddhartha said. "And once I learned this I consid-ered my life, and it too was a river, and the boy Siddhartha was separated from the man Siddhartha and the graybeard Sid-dhartha only by shadows, not by real things. Siddhartha's pre-vious lives were also not the past, and his death and his return to Brahman not the future. Nothing was, nothing will be; everything is, everything has being and presence."

Siddhartha spoke with rapture; this enlightenment had made him profoundly happy. Oh, was not then all suffering time, was not all self-torment and fear time, did not every-thing difficult, everything hostile in the world vanish, was it not overcome as soon as one had overcome time, as soon as one could think it out of existence? He had spoken in rapture, but Vasudeva smiled at him, beaming, and nodded in affirmation; he nodded silently, ran his hand across Siddhartha's shoulder, and turned back to his work.

On yet another occasion, when the river had swollen in monsoon season and was raging, Siddhartha said, "Isn't it true, my friend, that the river has many voices, very many voices? Does it not have the voice of a king, and of a warrior, and of a bull, and of a nocturnal bird, and of a woman giving birth, and of a man heaving a sigh, and a thousand voices more?"

"It is so." Vasudeva nodded. "All the voices of the creatures are in its voice."

"And do you know," Siddhartha went on, "what word it is the river is speaking when you succeed in hearing all its ten thousand voices at once?"

Vasudeva smiled happily; he leaned toward Siddhartha and spoke the holy *Om* into his ear. And this was just what Siddhartha had heard.

And each time Siddhartha smiled, his face became more and more like that of the ferryman, almost as beaming, almost as suffused with happiness, almost as shining from a thousand tiny wrinkles, as childish, as aged. Many travelers, seeing the two ferrymen together, took them for brothers. Often they sat together in the evenings beside the riverbank on the tree trunk, sat in silence, both listening to the water, which for them was not water but rather the voice of Life, the voice of Being, of the eternally Becoming. And from time to time it would happen that both of them, listening to the river, thought of the same things—of a conversation from the day before yesterday, of one of their travelers whose face and destiny occupied them, of death, of their childhoods—and both of them would glance at each other at just the same moment when the river had said something good to them, and both were thinking precisely the same thing; both men were glad about the same answer they had received to the same question.

There was something about the ferry and the two ferry-men that some travelers could feel. From time to time it would happen that a passenger, having looked into the face of one of the ferrymen, began to tell the story of his life, told of his sorrow, confessed to wicked deeds, asked for consolation or counsel. From time to time it would happen that someone asked for permission to spend an evening with them so as to listen to the river. It happened, too, that the curious came, people who had heard it said that this ferry was home to two wise men or magicians or saints. The curious asked many questions, but they received no answers, and they found nei-ther magicians nor wise men; they found only two old, friendly little men who appeared to be mute and somewhat odd and benighted. And the curious laughed and conversed with one another about how foolishly and credulously people spread such empty rumors.

The years passed without anyone counting them. Then one day monks arrived on a pilgrimage, disciples of Gautama, the Buddha, asking to be ferried across the river, and from them the ferrymen learned that they were journeying back to see their great teacher as swiftly as possible because the news had reached them that the Sublime One was gravely ill and would soon die his last human death and attain salvation. Not long after, another group of monks came to the ferry on their pilgrimage, and then another, and not only the monks but most of the other travelers and wanderers as well spoke of nothing but Gautama and his impending death. And just as people come streaming through the countryside from all directions to witness a military campaign or the coronation of a king—gathering here and there in little groups like ants—this is how they came streaming now, as if drawn by a magic spell, to where the great Buddha was awaiting his death, where this colossal event would take place and the great man of the epoch, the Perfect One, would go to his glory.

Siddhartha thought often in these days of the wise man on his deathbed, the great teacher whose voice had prevailed on entire peoples and roused hundreds of thousands, whose voice he too had once heard, whose holy countenance he too had once gazed upon with awe. He thought of him with affection, saw the path of his perfection in his mind's eye, and with a smile recalled the words with which he had once, as a young man, addressed the Sublime One. These words, it now appeared to him, had been proud and precocious; he smiled as he remembered them. A long time ago he had realized there was no longer anything separating him from Gautama, whose doctrine he had been unable to accept. No, a true seeker could not accept doctrine, not a seeker who truly wished to find. But the one who had found what he was seeking could give his approval to any teaching, any discipline at all, to any path, any goal—there was no longer anything separating him from the thousand others who were living in the Eternal and breathing the Divine.

On one of these days when so many were making pilgrimages to see the dying Buddha, Kamala was among the pilgrims: Kamala, once the most beautiful of courtesans. She had long since withdrawn from her former way of life, had given her garden to Gautama's monks, had taken refuge in his teachings, and was one of those women who provided for and gave friendship to the pilgrims. Together with the boy Siddhartha, her son, she had set out as soon as word of Gautama's impending death reached her, set out wearing simple clothes and on foot. She had been walking beside the river with her little son, but the boy soon grew tired and wanted to go home, wanted to rest, wanted to eat, became stubborn and tearful. Frequently Kamala had to stop with him; he was accustomed to having his way, and she had to feed him, console him, and scold him. He didn't understand why he was having to go on this exhausting, gloomy pilgrimage with his mother, having to go to a strange place to see a man he did not know who was holy and now lay dying. Let him die; what was it to the boy?

The pilgrims were approaching Vasudeva's ferry when little Siddhartha again forced his mother to stop and rest. Even Kamala was exhausted, and while the boy was chewing on a banana, she squatted down on the ground, closed her eyes for a little, and rested. But suddenly she gave a piteous wail. The boy looked at her, terrified, and saw her face ashen with horror; beneath her dress a small black snake darted out that had just bitten her.

Quickly the two of them raced down the path to get to where people were; not far from the ferry, Kamala collapsed, unable to go on. But the boy began wailing with misery, kissing and embracing his mother between his cries, and she too joined in his loud cries for help until the noise reached the ears of Vasudeva, who was standing beside the ferry. He ran up, took the woman in his arms, and carried her to the boat, the boy running alongside, and soon they all reached the hut where Siddhartha stood at the hearth, making a fire. He glanced up and saw first the face of the boy, which he found strangely evocative, reminiscent of things long forgotten. Then he saw Kamala, whom he recognized at once, though she lay unconscious in the arms of the ferryman, and now he knew it was his own son whose face had so struck him, and his heart stirred in his breast.

They washed Kamala's wound, but it was already black and her body swollen; they poured a medicinal drink between her lips. She came to again as she lay on Siddhartha's bed in the hut, and bending over her stood Siddhartha, who had once loved her. Thinking it all a dream, she gazed, smiling, into the face of her friend; only slowly, as the awareness of her circumstances returned to her, did she remember the bite and call out anxiously for the boy.

"He is here with you, do not worry," Siddhartha said.

Kamala looked into his eyes. Her tongue was heavy as she spoke, numbed by the poison. "You have grown old, my love," she said. "You have turned gray. But you resemble the young Samana who once came into my garden with no clothes on and with dust on his feet. You resemble him far more closely now than you did the day you left me, left Kamaswami. In your eyes you resemble him, Siddhartha. Oh, I too have grown old. Were you nonetheless able to recognize me?"

Siddhartha smiled. "I recognized you at once, Kamala, my love."

Kamala pointed to her boy and said, "Did you recognize him as well? He is your son."

She glanced about wildly, then her eyes fell shut. The boy began to cry. Siddhartha took him on his lap, let him cry, caressed his hair, and when he looked into the childish face he was reminded of a Brahmin prayer he had once learned when he himself was a small boy. Slowly, in a singsong voice, he began to recite it; the words came flooding back to him from the past, from childhood. And his chanting made the boy grow quiet; he now gave only the occasional sob, and then he fell asleep. Siddhartha laid him upon Vasudeva's bed. Vasudeva stood at the hearth, cooking rice. Siddhartha threw him a glance that he returned, smiling.

"She is going to die," Siddhartha said quietly.

Vasudeva nodded, the glow of the fire on the hearth flickering across his kind face.

Kamala regained consciousness one last time. Her face was contorted with pain; Siddhartha's eyes read the suffering on her lips, on her pallid cheeks. In silence he read it, attentively, waiting, immersed in her suffering. Kamala could feel this; her gaze sought his. Looking at him, she said, "Now I see that even your eyes have changed. They have become completely different. How am I still able to recognize that you are Siddhartha? You both are and are not."

Siddhartha did not speak; in silence his eyes met hers.

"Have you reached it?" she asked. "Have you found peace?"

He smiled and laid his hand upon hers.

"I can see you have," she said, "I can see it. I too will find peace."

"You have found it," Siddhartha said in a whisper.

Kamala gazed intently into his eyes. She thought about how she had wanted to make a pilgrimage to see Gautama in order to behold the face of a Perfect One, to breathe in his peace, and now she had found not Gautama but this man, and this was good, just as good as if she had seen the other one. She wanted to tell him this, but her tongue would no longer obey her will. Silently she gazed at him, and he watched as the life ebbed from her eyes. When the final agony had filled them and left them lifeless, when the final shudder had trembled through her body, he ran his fingers down her eyelids to close them.

For a long time he sat there, gazing at her face in its repose. For a long time he regarded her mouth, her old, weary mouth whose lips had grown narrow, and remembered that he had once, in the spring of his years, compared this mouth to a fig split in two. For a long time he sat there, reading this pallid face, these weary wrinkles, filling himself with the sight, and he saw his own face lying there in just the same way, just as white, just as lifeless, and at the same time saw his face and hers young again, with red lips and burning eyes, and the feeling of presence and simultaneity flooded through him, the feeling of eternity. He felt deeply in this hour, more deeply than ever before, the indestructibility of every life, the eternity of every moment.

When he stood up, Vasudeva had prepared rice for him,

but Siddhartha did not eat. In the lean-to where they kept their goat, the two old men spread out straw for themselves, and Vasudeva lay down to sleep. But Siddhartha went out and sat before the hut, listening to the river, with the past eddying around him, touched and enfolded by all the ages of his life at once. Only once, after a little while, did he get up, go to the door of the hut, and listen to make sure the boy was asleep.

Early the next morning, even before the sun had shown itself, Vasudeva emerged from the lean-to and joined his friend.

"You did not sleep," he said.

"No, Vasudeva. I sat here and listened to the river. It told me many things, filled me deeply with salutary thought, with the thought of Oneness."

"You have experienced sorrow, Siddhartha, yet I can see that no sadness has entered your heart."

"No, dear friend, how could I be sad? I, who was already rich and happy, have been made even richer and happier. My son has been given to me."

"I too welcome your son. But now, Siddhartha, let us set to work; there is much to do. Kamala died on the very bed where my wife died before her. Let us build Kamala's funeral pyre on the very same hill where I once built the pyre for my wife."

While the boy was still sleeping, they built the pyre.

THE SON

The boy had been shy and weeping as he attended his mother's funeral; he had been sullen and shy as he listened to Siddhartha, who greeted him as his son and bade him welcome in Vasudeva's hut. Pallid, he sat for days beside the dead woman's hillock, refused to eat, shut his eyes, and shut his heart, struggling against Fate, resisting it.

Siddhartha was gentle with him and let him do as he wished; he honored his grief. Siddhartha understood that his son did not know him, that he could not love him as a father. Slowly, too, he began to realize that this eleven-year-old was spoiled, a mama's boy; he had been raised among all the amenities of wealth and was used to fine meals, a soft bed, and giving orders to servants. Siddhartha understood that this spoiled, grief-stricken boy was utterly incapable of resigning himself suddenly and obligingly to an unfamiliar life of poverty, so he did not force him. He performed various chores for him, always saving him the choicest morsels. Slowly, he hoped, he would be able to win him over with kindness and patience.

Rich and happy is what he'd called himself when the boy

had come to him. But when with the passing of time the boy remained a sullen stranger, when he displayed a proud and stubborn heart, refused to work, showed no reverence for his elders, and plundered Vasudeva's fruit trees, Siddhartha began to understand that it was not happiness and peace that had come to him with his son but, rather, sorrow and worry. But he loved him and preferred the sorrow and worry of love to the happiness and peace he had known without the boy.

Since young Siddhartha's arrival in the hut, the two old men had split up their work. Vasudeva had once more begun to perform the duties of ferryman on his own, while Siddhartha, wanting to keep his son near him, took over the work in the hut and the field.

For a long time, for long months, Siddhartha waited for his son to understand him, to accept his love and perhaps even return it. For long months Vasudeva waited, observing this: waited and kept his peace. One day, when the boy Siddhartha had yet again tormented his father with his defiance and moods and had broken both rice bowls, Vasudeva took his friend aside in the evening and spoke with him.

"Forgive me," he said. "I am speaking to you with a friend's heart. I can see you are suffering, I can see you are troubled. Your son, my friend, is making you worry, and I also worry on his account. This young bird is accustomed to a different life, a different nest. Unlike you, he did not flee from wealth, from the city, out of nausea and surfeit; he was forced to leave them behind against his will. I have asked the river, my friend; many times I have asked it. But the river only laughs—it laughs at me, both at me and at you, shakes with laughter at our foolishness. Water seeks out water; youth seeks out youth. Your son is not in a place where he can flourish. Ask the river and hear its counsel for yourself!"

Distressed, Siddhartha gazed into Vasudeva's kind face, in whose many furrows a constant gaiety resided.

"Could I bring myself to part with him?" he asked quietly, ashamed. "Give me more time, my friend! I am fighting for him, you see, trying to win his heart and hoping to capture it with loving-kindness and patience. To him too the river must speak someday; he too has a calling."

Vasudeva's smile blossomed more warmly. "Indeed, he too has a calling; he too will enjoy eternal life. But do we know, you and I, to what he has been called: to what path, to what deeds, to what sufferings? His sorrows will not be slight, for his heart is proud and hard; those like him must suffer a great deal, commit many errors, do much wrong, pile much sin upon themselves. Tell me, my friend, are you educating your son? Do you force him? Do you strike him? Do you punish him?"

"No, Vasudeva, I do none of these things."

"This I knew. You do not force him, do not strike him, do not command him because you know that soft is stronger than hard, water stronger than rock, love stronger than violence. Very good, I praise you. But is it not an error for you to think that you are not forcing him, not punishing him? Do you not bind him with the bands of your love? Do you not shame him daily and make things more difficult for him with your kindness and patience? Are you not forcing him, the arrogant and spoiled boy, to live in a hut with two old banana eaters for whom even rice is a delicacy, whose thoughts cannot be his, whose hearts are old and still and beat differently from his? Do all these things not force him, punish him?"

In dismay, Siddhartha cast his eyes down. Softly he asked, "What do you think I should do?"

Vasudeva said, "Take him to the city, to his mother's house. There will still be servants there; give him to them. And if there is no one left, take him to a teacher, not because of what he will learn but because he will then be among other boys and girls, in the world where he belongs. Have you never thought of this?"

"You have seen into my heart," Siddhartha said sadly. "Often I have thought of this. But tell me, how can I release him into this world when his heart is so ungentle to begin with? Will he not become a hedonist, will he not lose himself in pleasure and power, will he not repeat all his father's errors, will he not become perhaps forever lost in Sansara?"

The ferryman's smile radiated brightness; he touched Siddhartha's arm gently and said, "Ask the river, my friend! Listen to its laughter! Or do you really believe that you committed your own follies so as to spare your son from committing them? And will you be able to save your son from Sansara? How, with doctrine, with prayer, with admonitions? My friend, have you entirely forgotten that instructive story about Siddhartha, the Brahmin's son, that you once related to me here in this very spot? Who saved the Samana Siddhartha from Sansara, from sin, from greed, from folly? Were his father's piety, his teachers' admonitions, his own knowledge, and his own searching able to protect him? What father, what teacher, was able to protect him from living life himself, soiling himself with life, accumulating guilt, drinking the bitter drink, finding his own path? Do you think then, my friend, that this path might be spared anyone at all? Perhaps your little son, because you love him and would like to spare him sorrow and pain and disillusionment? But even if you died ten times for him, you would not succeed in relieving him of even the smallest fraction of his destiny."

Never before had Vasudeva spoken so many words at once. Siddhartha thanked him warmly, went into the hut with his heart full of worry, and for a long time could not find sleep. Vasudeva had told him nothing that he himself had not already thought and known. But it was a knowledge he could not act on; stronger than this knowledge was his love for the boy, his tenderness, his fear of losing him. Had he ever given his heart so completely to anything, had he ever loved another person so deeply, so blindly, with so much suffering, with so little success and yet so happily?

Siddhartha was unable to follow his friend's advice; he could not give up his son. He allowed the boy to order him about and treat him with contempt. He kept his peace and waited, each day recommencing the silent battle of kindness, the soundless war of patience. Vasudeva also waited and held his peace, in kindness, wisdom, and forbearance. In patience, both of them were masters.

Once when the boy's face reminded him very much of Kamala, Siddhartha suddenly remembered something Kamala had once said to him a long time before, in the days of their youth. "You cannot love," she had said, and he had agreed that she was right, comparing himself to a star and the child people to falling leaves; nonetheless, he had felt a reproach in what she'd said. It was true that he had never been able to lose himself entirely in another person, give himself to another, forget himself, commit the follies of love for the sake of another; never had he been able to do this—and this, it had seemed to him at the time, was the great difference separating him from the child people. But now, ever since his son had come, he, Siddhartha, had become a child person in his own right, suffering because of another person, loving another person, lost, a fool, because of love. Now he too felt for once in his life, late as it was, this strongest and strangest of passions, was suffering because of it, suffering terribly, and yet he was blissful; he felt somehow renewed, somehow richer.

He could sense quite distinctly that this blind love for his son was a passion, something very human, that it was Sansara, a muddy spring, dark water. Yet at the same time he felt that it was not without value—it was necessary, it came out of his own being. This too was pleasure that had to be atoned for;

this too, pain to be experienced; these too, follies to be committed.

Meanwhile, his son let him go on committing these follies, let him go on trying to win him over, let him humble himself daily before his moods. There was nothing about this father to delight him, nothing he might have feared. He was a good man, this father, a good, kind, gentle man, very pious perhaps, perhaps a saint—none of these were traits that might have served to win the boy's heart. What a bore this father was, keeping him trapped in this miserable hut, a bore who received all sorts of bad behavior with a smile, responded to insults with amicability and to wicked deeds with kindness. This was the old hypocrite's most contemptible trick. The boy would have much preferred to be threatened and mistreated.

The day arrived when young Siddhartha's volition reached the bursting point and he turned openly against his father. Siddhartha had given the boy a task. He was to go collect brushwood. But the boy did not leave the hut; he remained standing there, defiant and furious, stamping the floor and balling up his fists, and in a violent outburst he shouted his hatred and contempt into his father's face.

"Go fetch your brushwood yourself!" he cried, seething. "I am not your servant! I know you will not strike me, you wouldn't dare; I know you are constantly trying to punish me and belittle me with your piousness and forbearance. You want me to become just like you, just as pious, just as gentle, just as wise! I, on the other hand—mark my words!—would rather, just to spite you, become a highwayman and murderer and go to hell than be like you! I hate you! You are not my father, even if you were my mother's lover ten times over!"

Anger and grief overflowed in him, bubbling up in a hundred harsh and wicked words directed at his father. Then the boy ran off and did not return until late in the evening.

The next morning, however, he was gone. Gone too was a

small basket, woven of two shades of bast fiber, in which the ferrymen kept the copper and silver coins they received for their services. Gone too was the boat; Siddhartha saw it lying on the opposite shore. The boy had run away.

"I have to follow him," said Siddhartha, who had been trembling with misery since the boy's outburst the day before. "A child cannot walk through the forest all alone. He will perish. We have to build a raft, Vasudeva, to get across the water."

"We will build a raft," Vasudeva said, "in order to retrieve our boat, which the boy has taken. But as for the boy himself, you should let him go, my friend. He is no longer a child; he can look after himself. He is trying to make his way back to the city, and he is right to do so, remember this. He is doing what you yourself failed to do. He is providing for himself, choosing his own path. Oh, Siddhartha, I can see that you are suffering, but this is pain of a sort that is tempting to laugh about—even you will soon be laughing at it!"

Siddhartha did not respond. He already held the ax in his hand and was beginning to make a raft out of bamboo, and Vasudeva helped him bind the trunks together with grass rope. Then they crossed to the other side, drifting far downstream, and pulled the raft back up along the opposite shore.

"Why did you bring the ax with you?" Siddhartha asked.

Vasudeva said, "It is possible that our boat's oar might be lost."

Siddhartha knew what his friend was thinking. He thought the boy would have thrown away or broken the oar to avenge himself and keep them from following him. And indeed there was no longer an oar in the boat. Vasudeva pointed to the bottom of the boat and looked at his friend with a smile, as if to say, See what your son is trying to tell you? See that he wishes not to be followed? But he did not say this in words. He set about constructing a new oar. Siddhartha, however, took leave of him in order to search for the runaway. Vasudeva did not stop him.

Siddhartha had been hurrying through the forest for a long time when it occurred to him that his search was in vain. Either the boy was far ahead of him and had already reached the city, he thought, or, if he was still on his way, he would hide from his pursuer. As he continued to think, he realized that he was not in truth worried about his son; in his heart he knew that the boy neither had perished nor was threatened by dangers in the forest. Nonetheless, he continued to run without stopping, no longer because he wished to rescue the boy but merely out of desire, in the hope of perhaps seeing him once more. And he ran all the way to the outskirts of the city.

When he reached the main road just outside town, he remained standing at the entrance to the beautiful pleasure garden that had belonged to Kamala, where he had seen her for the first time, sitting in her sedan chair. What once had been now stirred again in his soul. Once more he saw himself standing there, young, a bearded naked Samana, his hair full of dust. For a long time Siddhartha stood there gazing through the open gate into the garden, where monks in yellow robes walked beneath the beautiful trees.

For a long time he stood there reflecting, seeing images, hearing the tale of his own life. For a long time he stood there gazing at the monks, seeing instead of them the young man Siddhartha, seeing young Kamala strolling beneath the lofty trees. Distinctly he saw himself being served food and drink by Kamala, receiving her first kiss, looking back with pride and scorn upon his life as a Brahmin, and filled with pride and desire as he began his worldly life. He saw Kamaswami, saw the servants, saw the banquets, the dice players, the musicians, saw Kamala's songbird in its cage, lived all these things over again, breathed Sansara, was once more old and weary, once more felt the nausea, felt the desire to extinguish himself, and once more recovered thanks to the holy *Om*.

After he had stood for a long time beside the gate to the garden, Siddhartha realized it had been a foolish desire that had driven him to this place. He could not help his son and he should not cling to him. Deeply he felt his love for the runaway boy in his heart—it was like a wound—yet at the same time he felt that this wound had not been given him that he might wallow in it: This wound was to be a radiant blossom.

That his wound was not yet blossoming, not yet radiant, made him sad. In place of his goal, the object of the desires that had drawn him here, drawn him to follow his runaway son, he found only emptiness. Sadly he sat down, felt something dying in his heart, felt emptiness, no longer saw any joy before him, any goal. Immersed in these thoughts, he sat and waited. This he had learned beside the river, this one thing: to wait, to be patient, to listen. And he sat there listening in the dust of the road, listening to his heart beating wearily and sadly, waiting for a voice. For hours he squatted there listening, no longer seeing any images, sinking into the emptiness, letting himself sink with no path before his eyes. And when he felt his wound stinging, he soundlessly pronounced the word *Om*, filled himself with *Om*. The monks in the garden saw him, and as he remained squatting there for many hours, the dust collecting in his gray hair, one of them came up and placed two pisang fruits beside him. The old man did not notice.

From this paralysis he was awakened by a hand touching his shoulder. Instantly recognizing this touch, gentle and modest, he came to again. He stood up and greeted Vasudeva, who had come after him. And when he gazed into Vasudeva's kind face, gazed at the little wrinkles that looked as if they were bursting with laughter, gazed into his merry eyes, he smiled as well. Now he saw the pisang fruits lying before him; he picked them up, gave one to the ferryman, and ate the other himself. Then, without a word, he accompanied Vasudeva back into the woods and returned home to the ferry.

Neither spoke of what had taken place that day, neither spoke the name of the boy, neither spoke of his flight, neither spoke of the wound. In the hut, Siddhartha lay down on his bed and when, some time later, Vasudeva came to his bedside to offer him a bowl of coconut milk, he found him already sleeping.

Oм

For a long time his wound continued to smart. A number of the travelers Siddhartha ferried across the river had a son or daughter with them, and he was never able to look at them without feeling envy, without thinking, So many, many thousands enjoy this most precious sort of happiness; why can't I? Even wicked people, even thieves and robbers have children and love them and are loved by them; I alone do not. How simple his thoughts had now become, how lacking in understanding. That's how greatly he had come to resemble the child people.

He now saw people differently than he had before, less cleverly, less proudly, but more warmly, with more curiosity and empathy. When he ferried ordinary sorts of people across the river, child people, tradespeople, warriors, womenfolk, they did not appear so strange to him as once they had; he understood them. He shared their life, which was governed not by thoughts and insights but by drives and desires; he felt like one of them. Although he had nearly reached perfection and still felt the pangs of his recent wound, it seemed to him as if these child people were his brothers. Their vanities, desires, and ridiculous habits were losing their ridiculousness for him; they were becoming comprehensible, lovable, even worthy of respect. A mother's blind love for her child, a self-satisfied father's blind pride in his one little son, a vain young woman's blind, furious urge to bedeck herself with jewels and attract men's admiring glances—all these drives, all these childish matters, all these simple, foolish, but enormously strong, strongly alive, strongly asserted drives and desires were no longer mere child's play to Siddhartha; he saw people living for their sake, saw them performing endless feats for their sake—making journeys, waging wars, suffering endless sufferings, enduring endless burdens—and he was able to love them for this; he saw life, the living, the indestructible, the Brahman in each of their passions, each of their deeds. Lovable and admirable these people were in their blind fidelity, their blind strength and tenacity. They were lacking in almost nothing; the one thing possessed by the thinker, the man of knowledge, that they lacked was only a trifle, one small thing: consciousness, conscious thought of the Oneness of all things. And at times Siddhartha even doubted whether this knowledge, this thinking, should be so highly valued, wondered whether it too was not perhaps the child's play of thought people, who might be the child people of thought. In all other matters, the worldly were the wise man's equals, were in fact far superior to him in many ways, just as animals, in their tenacious, unerring performance of what is necessary, can appear superior to people at certain moments.

Slowly blossoming, slowly ripening within Siddhartha, was the realization and knowledge of what wisdom and the goal of his long search really was. It was nothing but a readiness of the soul, a capacity, the secret art of being able at every moment, without ceasing to live, to think the thought of Oneness, to feel Oneness and breathe it in. Slowly this was blossoming within him, shining out at him from Vasudeva's aged childish face: harmony, knowledge of the eternal perfection of the world, smiling, Oneness.

His wound, however, continued to smart. With longing and bitterness Siddhartha thought of his son, nurtured the love and tenderness in his heart, allowed the pain to gnaw at him, committed all the follies of love. This was a flame that would not go out of its own accord.

One day when the wound was violently burning, Siddhartha crossed the river, driven by longing, got out of the boat, and was of a mind to go to the city again and look for his son. The river was flowing gently and softly; it was the dry season, but its voice sounded odd; it was laughing! It was distinctly laughing. The river was laughing, brightly and clearly laughing at the old ferryman. Siddhartha stopped. He leaned over the water to hear better and saw his face reflected in the calm streaming water, and in this mirrored face there was something that stirred his memory, something forgotten, and when he considered further, he realized what it was: This face resembled another face he had once known and loved and also feared. It resembled the face of his father, the Brahmin. And he remembered how, a very long time ago, he, a mere youth, had forced his father to let him go to join the penitents, how he had taken leave of him, and then he had gone and had never again returned. Had not his father suffered the same pain he himself was now suffering on account of his son? Had not his father died long ago, without ever having seen his son again? Must not he himself expect the same fate? Was not this repetition a comedy, a strange and foolish thing, this constant circulation in a preordained course?

The river laughed. Yes, it was true, everything returned again that had not been fully suffered and resolved; it was always the same sorrows being suffered over and over. Siddhartha, however, climbed into the boat again and crossed back over to where the hut was with the river laughing at him, thinking of his father, thinking of his son, locked in battle with himself, feeling inclined to plunge into despair but equally inclined to join in this laughter at himself and all the world. Oh, his wound had not yet blossomed; his heart was still struggling against fate; merriment and victory did not yet shine from his sorrow. But he did feel hope, and when he had returned to the hut, he felt an unconquerable desire to reveal himself to Vasudeva, to show him everything, tell everything to him, the master listener.

Vasudeva was sitting in the hut weaving a basket. He no longer operated the ferry. His eyes were beginning to grow weak, and not only his eyes but his arms and hands as well. Alone unchanged and blossoming were the joy and the gay benevolence of his face.

Siddhartha sat down beside the old man and slowly began to speak. Things they had never said before, of these he now spoke, telling of the journey he had made to the city, of his stinging wound, of his envy when he beheld happy fathers, of his knowledge of the foolishness of such desires, of struggling in vain to resist them. All these things he now recounted; he was able to speak of all of them, even the most embarrassing things. Everything could be told, everything displayed; he could say all of it. He showed Vasudeva his wound and also told the story of his flight that day, of his crossing the river, a childish refugee intending to journey on to the city, and how the river had laughed.

He spoke for a long time, and as Vasudeva listened with his still face, Siddhartha felt Vasudeva's listening more strongly than ever before. He could sense how his pain and his anxieties were flowing away from him, felt his secret hopes flow away and then come back toward him from the other side. Showing this listener his wound was just the same as bathing it in the river until it became cool and one with the water. As he continued to speak, continued to confess and recount, Siddhartha felt more and more strongly that it was no longer Vasudeva listening to him, no longer a human being, that this motionless listener was drinking in his confession as a tree drinks in rain, that this motionless one was the river, God, the Eternal itself. And as Siddhartha ceased to think of himself and his wound, his recognition of the changed essence of Vasudeva took possession of him; the more deeply he felt it and entered into it, the less strange it became and the more he realized that all this was as it should be and natural, that Vasudeva had been this way a long time, nearly always; it was just that he himself had not quite recognized it, and that in fact he himself was scarcely different from Vasudeva any longer. He became aware that he was now seeing old Vasudeva the way people see the gods, and that this could not go on indefinitely; in his heart he began to take leave of Vasudeva. All this time he was continuing to speak.

When he had finished, Vasudeva fixed his kind and now somewhat feeble gaze upon him without speaking, silently radiating love and gaiety in his direction, understanding and knowledge. He took Siddhartha's hand, led him to their seat on the riverbank, sat down there with him, and smiled at the river.

"You have heard the river laugh," he said, "but you have not heard everything. Let us listen; you will hear more."

They listened. Gently, the many-voiced song of the river rang out. Siddhartha gazed into the streaming water, and in the water images appeared to him—his father appeared, lonely, mourning for his son; he himself appeared, lonely, and also bound to his distant son with the bands of longing; his son appeared, himself lonely, the boy eagerly storming down the flaming path of his young desires—each one with his sights set on his own goal, each one possessed by his goal, each one suffering. The river sang with a voice of sorrow; it sang longingly, and longingly it flowed on toward its goal, its voice a lament.

Do you hear? Vasudeva's mute gaze asked. Siddhartha nodded. "Listen better!" Vasudeva whispered.

Siddhartha made an effort to listen better. The image of his father, his own image, and the image of his son all flowed together; Kamala's image also appeared and dissolved, and the image of Govinda, and other images; they all flowed together. All became the river, all of them striving as river to reach their goal, longingly, eagerly, suffering, and the river's voice rang out full of longing, full of burning sorrow, full of unquenchable desire. The river strove to its goal; Siddhartha saw it hurrying along, the river that was made of himself and those he loved and all the people he had ever seen; all the waves and waters were hurrying, suffering, toward goals, many goals—the waterfall, the lake, the rapids, the sea—and all these goals were reached, and each of them was followed by a new goal, and the water turned to steam and rose into the sky; it became rain and plunged down from the heavens; it became a spring, became a brook, became a river, striving anew, flowing anew. But the longing voice had changed. It still rang out, sorrowfully, searchingly, but other voices now joined it, voices of joy and of sorrow, good and wicked voices, laughing and mourning, a hundred voices, a thousand.

Siddhartha listened. He was now completely and utterly immersed in his listening, utterly empty, utterly receptive; he felt he had now succeeded in learning how to listen. He had heard all these things often now, these many voices in the river; today it sounded new. Already he could no longer distinguish the many voices, could not distinguish the gay from the weeping, the childish from the virile; they all belonged together, the yearning laments and the wise man's laughter, the cry of anger and the moans of the dying; they were all one, all of them interlinked and interwoven, bound together in a thousand ways. And all of this together—all the voices, all the goals, all the longing, all the suffering, all the pleasure, everything good and everything bad—all of it together was the world. All of it together was the river of occurrences, the music of life. And when Siddhartha listened attentively to this river, to this thousand-voiced song, when he listened neither for the sorrow nor for the laughter, when he did not attach his soul to any one voice and enter into it with his ego but rather heard all of them, heard the whole, the oneness—then the great song of the thousand voices consisted only of a single word: *Om*, perfection.

Do you hear? Vasudeva's gaze asked once more.

Vasudeva's smile gleamed brightly; over the furrows of his aged countenance floated a luminous radiance, just as the *Om* floated radiant above all the voices of the river. His smile gleamed as he regarded his friend, and now Siddhartha's face too gleamed brightly with the same smile. His wound blossomed; his sorrow shone; his Self had flowed into the Oneness.

In this hour Siddhartha ceased to do battle with fate, ceased to suffer. Upon his face blossomed the gaiety of knowledge that is no longer opposed by any will, that knows perfection, that is in agreement with the river of occurrences, with the current of life, full of empathy, full of fellow feeling, given over to the current, part of the Oneness.

When Vasudeva arose from his seat on the riverbank, when he looked into Siddhartha's eyes and saw the gaiety of knowledge gleaming in them, he touched his friend's shoulder quietly with his hand in his careful and tender way and said, "I have waited for this hour, dearest friend. Now that it has come, let me go. For a long time I have waited, for a long time I have been the ferryman Vasudeva. Now it is enough. Farewell, hut; farewell, river; farewell, Siddhartha!"

Siddhartha bowed deeply before the one taking his leave.

"I knew this," he said softly. "You will go into the forest?"

"I am going into the forest; I am going into Oneness," said Vasudeva, radiant.

Radiant, he departed; Siddhartha watched him go. With deep joy, with deep solemnity he watched him go: saw each of his steps full of peace, saw his head full of splendor, saw his figure full of light.

GOVINDA

In the company of other monks, Govinda once rested on one of his journeys in the pleasure grove that the courtesan Kamala had given to the disciples of Gautama. There he heard tell of an old ferryman who lived a day's journey away beside the river and was considered by many to be a wise man. When it was time for Govinda to continue on his way, he chose the path to the ferry, eager to see this ferryman. For although he had lived all his life according to the rules and was regarded with reverence by the younger monks on account of his age and his modesty, the restlessness and searching had not yet been extinguished in his heart.

He went to the river and asked the old man to take him across, and when they got out of the boat on the opposite shore, he said, "You have shown us monks and pilgrims much kindness; many of us have been ferried across the river by you. Are you not also, ferryman, a seeker in search of the right path?"

Siddhartha, his old eyes smiling, said, "You call yourself a seeker, O Venerable One, and yet are advanced in years and wear the robe of the monks of Gautama?"

"Indeed, I am old," Govinda said, "but I have not stopped

searching. Never will I cease to search; this seems to be my destiny. You too, it seems to me, have done some searching. Will you speak a word to me, Revered One?"

Siddhartha said, "What could I have to say to you, Venerable One? Perhaps this, that you are seeking all too much? That all your seeking is making you unable to find?"

"How is this?" Govinda asked.

"When a person seeks," Siddhartha said, "it can easily happen that his eye sees only the thing he is seeking; he is incapable of finding anything, of allowing anything to enter into him, because he is always thinking only of what he is looking for, because he has a goal, because he is possessed by his goal. Seeking means having a goal. Finding means being free, being open, having no goal. You, Venerable One, are perhaps indeed a seeker, for, striving to reach your goal, you overlook many things that lie close before your eyes."

"I don't quite understand yet," Govinda said. "How do you mean this?"

Siddhartha replied, "Once, O Venerable One, many years ago, you came to this river, and beside the river found a sleeping man, and you sat down beside him to watch over his sleep. But you did not, O Govinda, recognize the sleeper."

Astonished, like a man bewitched, the monk looked into the ferryman's eyes.

"Are you Siddhartha?" he asked, his voice shy. "I would not have recognized you this time, either! With all my heart I greet you, Siddhartha, and am delighted to see you once more! You have changed a great deal, my friend. And so now you have become a ferryman?"

Siddhartha gave a friendly laugh. "A ferryman, yes. Some people, Govinda, have to change a great deal, have to wear all sorts of garments, and I am one of these, my dear friend. I welcome you, Govinda; come spend the night in my hut."

Govinda spent the night in the hut and slept upon the bed

that had once belonged to Vasudeva. He had many questions for the friend of his youth; Siddhartha had to tell him many things.

When, the next morning, it was time for Govinda to set off again on his day's journey, he said these words, not without hesitation: "Before I set off on my way again, Siddhartha, allow me one last question. Do you have a doctrine? Is there a belief or some knowledge that guides you, that helps you to live and do what is right?"

Said Siddhartha, "As you know, my dear friend, I began to distrust doctrines and teachers already as a young man, in the days when we were living among the penitents in the forest, and I turned my back on them. I have stuck to this. Nonetheless I have had many teachers since then. A beautiful courtesan was my teacher for a long time, and a wealthy merchant was my teacher, and a few dice players. Once, even an itinerant disciple of the Buddha was my teacher; he sat beside me when I had fallen asleep in the forest on a pilgrimage. From him as well I learned; to him as well I am grateful, very grateful. Most of all, however, I learned here, from this river, and from my predecessor, the ferryman Vasudeva. He was a very simple man, Vasudeva. He was not a thinker, but he knew what is necessary to know; just as much as Gautama he was a Perfect One, a saint."

Govinda said, "Even now, Siddhartha, you retain some fondness for mockery, it seems to me. I believe you and know that you never followed a teacher. But have you not yourself found, if not a doctrine, then at least certain thoughts, certain insights that belong to you and help you to live? If you were able to tell me something of them, you would fill my heart with joy."

Said Siddhartha, "I have had thoughts, yes, and insights, now and again. Sometimes, for an hour or a day, I have felt knowledge within me, just as one feels life within one's heart. There were several thoughts, but it would be difficult for me to hand them on to you. You see, my Govinda, here is one of the thoughts I have found: Wisdom cannot be passed on. Wisdom that a wise man attempts to pass on always sounds like foolishness."

"Do you speak in jest?" Govinda asked.

"It is no jest. I am saying what I have found. One can pass on knowledge but not wisdom. One can find wisdom, one can live it, one can be supported by it, one can work wonders with it, but one cannot speak it or teach it. I sometimes suspected this even as a youth; it is what drove me from my teachers. I have found a thought, Govinda, that you will think neither a joke nor foolishness; it is my best thought. It says: The opposite of every truth is just as true! For this is so: A truth can always only be uttered and cloaked in words when it is one-sided. Everything is one-sided that can be thought in thoughts and said with words, everything one-sided, everything half, everything is lacking wholeness, roundness, oneness. When the sublime Gautama spoke of the world in his doctrine, he had to divide it into Sansara and Nirvana, into illusion and truth, into suffering and redemption. This is the only way to go about it; there is no other way for a person who would teach. The world itself, however, the Being all around us and within us, is never one-sided. Never is a person, or a deed, purely Sansara or purely Nirvana, never is a person utterly holy or utterly sinful. It only seems so because we are subject to the illusion that time exists as something real. Time is not real, Govinda. I have experienced this again and again. And if time is not real, then the distance that appears to lie between world and eternity, between suffering and bliss, between evil and good, is also an illusion."

"How can this be?" Govinda asked anxiously.

"Listen well, my dear friend, listen well! The sinner who I am and who you are is a sinner, but one day he will again be Brahman, he will one day reach Nirvana, will be a Buddha— and now behold: This *one day* is an illusion, it is only an allegory! The sinner is not on his way to the state of Buddhahood, he is not caught up in a process of developing, although our thought cannot imagine things in any other way. No, in this sinner the future Buddha already exists—now, today—all his future is already there. In him, in yourself, in everyone you must worship the future Buddha, the potential Buddha, the hidden Buddha. The world, friend Govinda, is not imperfect, nor is it in the middle of a long path to perfection. No, it is perfect in every moment; every sin already carries forgiveness within it, all little children already carry their aged forms within them, all infants death, all dying men eternal life. It is not possible for anyone to see how far any other person has come along his path. Buddha waits within the robber and the dice player, and the robber waits in the Brahmin. In the deepest meditation we have the possibility of negating time, of seeing all life, all having-been, being, and becoming, as simultaneous, and then everything is good, everything is perfect, everything is Brahman. Therefore everything that *is* appears good to me. Death appears to me like life, sin like holiness, cleverness like folly; everything must be just as it is, everything requires only my assent, only my willingness, my loving approval, and for me it is good and can never harm me. I experienced by observing my own body and my own soul that I sorely needed sin, sorely needed concupiscence, needed greed, vanity, and the most shameful despair to learn to stop resisting, to learn to love the world and stop comparing it to some world I only wished for and imagined, some sort of perfection I myself had dreamed up, but instead to let it be as it was and to love it and be happy to belong to it.

"These, O Govinda, are a few of the thoughts that have come into my mind."

Siddhartha bent down, picked up a stone from the ground, and weighed it in his hand.

"This here," he said, playing with it, "is a stone, and in a certain amount of time it will perhaps be earth and from earth it will become a plant or an animal or man. Earlier I would have said, 'This stone is just a stone, it is worthless, it belongs to the world of Maya; but since in the cycle of transformations it might even become human and spirit, I must give it due consideration.' This is how I might have thought once. Today, however, I think, This stone is a stone; it is also animal, it is also God, it is also Buddha. I do not honor it and love it because it might one day become this or that, but because it already and always *is* all things—and precisely this—that it is a stone, that it appears to me now and today as a stone— precisely this is the reason I love it and see value and meaning in each of its veins and hollows, in the yellow, in the gray, in the hardness, in the sound it gives off when I knock on it, in the dryness or moistness of its surface. There are stones that feel like oil or soap, others that feel like leaves, others like sand, and each one is special and prays *Om* in its own way, each is Brahman, but at the same time and to just as great an extent, each one is a stone, is oily or soapy, and precisely this pleases me and seems to me wondrous and deserving of worship.

"But let me speak no more of this. Words are not good for the secret meaning; everything always becomes a little bit different the moment one speaks it aloud, a bit falsified, a bit foolish—yes, and this too is also very good and pleases me greatly: that one person's treasure and wisdom always sounds like foolishness to others."

Without a word, Govinda listened. "Why did you tell me all that about the stone?" he asked hesitantly, after a pause.

"This happened unintentionally. Or perhaps what was meant was this: For the stone and the river, for all these things that we contemplate and from which we can learn, I feel love. I can love a stone, Govinda, and also a tree or a piece of bark. These are things and things can be loved. Words, however, I cannot love. This is why doctrines are not for me. They have no hardness, no softness, no colors, no edges, no smell, no taste; they have nothing but words. Perhaps it is this that has hindered you in finding peace; perhaps it is all these words. For even redemption and virtue, even Sansara and Nirvana, are just words, Govinda. There is no thing that could *be* Nirvana; there is only the word Nirvana."

Govinda said, "Nirvana is not only a word, friend. It is a thought."

Siddhartha continued. "A thought—this may be true. I have to confess to you, my dear friend, I do not see much difference between thoughts and words. To speak plainly, I do not have such a high regard for thoughts, either. I have a much higher regard for things. Here on this ferryboat, for example, my predecessor and teacher was a man, a holy man, who for many years believed only in the river, nothing else. He noticed that the river's voice was speaking to him, and from this voice he learned; it taught and educated him. The river seemed to him a god, and for many years he did not know that every wind, every cloud, every bird, every beetle is just as divine and knows just as much and can teach just as much as the river he so revered. But when this holy man went into the forest, he knew everything, knew more than you or I, without teachers, without books, only because he had believed in the river."

Govinda said, "But what is it you are calling *things* if not real things, things that have being? Is this not merely an illusion of Maya, merely image and semblance? Your stone, your tree, your river—are they realities?"

"This too," Siddhartha said, "concerns me little. Let the things be semblances or not; then I too am only semblance, and so they will always be like me. This is what makes them so dear to me, makes me so admire them: They are like me. This is why I can love them. And here now is a bit of doctrine that will make you laugh: Love, O Govinda, appears to me more important than all other matters. To see through the world, to explain it, to scorn it—this may be the business of great thinkers. But what interests me is being able to love the world, not scorn it, not to hate it and hate myself, but to look at it and myself and all beings with love and admiration and reverence."

"This I understand," Govinda said. "But it is precisely this that he, the Sublime One, recognized as illusion. He commands benevolence, gentleness, pity, tolerance, but not love; he forbade us to bind our heart with love for earthly things."

"I know," Siddhartha said; his smile was radiant, golden. "I know, Govinda. And behold: Here we are in the middle of the thicket of opinions, in a battle over words. For I cannot deny that my words about love stand in opposition, in apparent opposition to Gautama's words. This is precisely why I distrust words so much, for I know this opposition is an illusion. I know I am in agreement with Gautama. How could he not know love, he who recognized all humanity in its transitoriness, its insignificance, and nonetheless loved human beings so much that he devoted a long, laborious life to the sole purpose of helping them, teaching them? Even with regard to him, your great teacher, things are dearer to me than words, his actions and life more important than his speeches, the gestures of his hand more important than his opinions. It is not in his speaking or in his thinking that I see his greatness, only in his actions, his life."

For a long time, the two old men were silent. Then Govinda said, bowing as he prepared to take leave of him, "Thank you, Siddhartha, for telling me something of your thoughts. They are in part strange thoughts; not all of them were immediately comprehensible to me. May this be as it will. I thank you and wish you peaceful days."

Secretly, however, he was thinking, What an odd person this Siddhartha is! These thoughts he is uttering are odd, and his doctrine sounds silly. The pure doctrine of the Sublime

One is so different from this, so much clearer, purer, more comprehensible, with nothing strange, silly, or ridiculous about it. But Siddhartha's hands and feet, his eyes, his brow, his breathing, his smiling, his way of greeting me, his gait seem to me quite different from his thoughts. Never since our sublime Gautama entered Nirvana, never since have I met a person who made me feel: This is a saint! He alone, this Siddhartha, has seemed a saint to me. His doctrine may be strange, his words may sound silly, but his gaze and his hand, his skin and his hair, everything about him radiates a purity, radiates a calm, radiates a gaiety and kindness and holiness that I have beheld in no other person since the final death of our sublime teacher.

As Govinda was thinking these things, his heart filled with conflict. He bent over once more to Siddhartha, drawn by love, and bowed deeply before the one sitting quietly beside him.

"Siddhartha," he said, "we have become old men. It is unlikely that either of us will ever see the other again in this shape. I can see, beloved friend, that you have found peace. I confess that I myself have not done so. Grant me just one word more, O Revered One; give me something that I can grasp, that I can comprehend! Give me something to take with me when we part. My path is often difficult, Siddhartha, often dark."

Siddhartha remained silent and continued to gaze at him with the same still smile. Govinda stared into his face with fear, with longing. Suffering and eternal searching stood written in his gaze, eternal not-finding.

Siddhartha saw this and smiled.

"Bend down to me," he whispered softly in Govinda's ear. "Bend down here to me! Yes, like that, closer! Even closer! Kiss me on the forehead, Govinda!"

When Govinda, perplexed and yet drawn by great love and foreboding, obeyed his words, bent down close to him, and touched his forehead with his lips, something wondrous happened to him. While his thoughts were still lingering over Siddhartha's odd words, while he was still fruitlessly and reluctantly attempting to think away time, to imagine Nirvana and Sansara as one, while a certain contempt for his friend's words was even then battling inside him with tremendous love and reverence, this happened:

He no longer saw the face of his friend Siddhartha; instead he saw other faces, many of them, a long series, a flowing river of faces, by the hundreds, by the thousands, all of them coming and fading away, and yet all of them appearing to be there at once, all of them constantly changing, being renewed, and all of them at the same time Siddhartha. He saw the face of a fish, a carp, its mouth wrenched open in infinite pain, a dying fish with dying eyes—he saw the face of a newborn child, red and full of wrinkles, all twisted up to cry—he saw the face of a murderer, saw him stick a knife into a person's body, and saw, at the same instant, this criminal kneeling down in chains and having his head chopped off by an executioner with one stroke of the sword—he saw the bodies of men and women naked in the positions and struggles of furious love—he saw corpses laid out, still, cold, empty—he saw the heads of animals: wild boars, crocodiles, elephants, bulls, birds—he saw gods, saw Krishna, saw Agni—he saw all these figures and faces in their thousandfold interrelations, each helping the others, loving them, hating them, destroying them, giving birth to them anew; each one was a wanting-to-die, a passionately painful confession of transitoriness, and yet none of them died; each of them was only transformed, constantly born anew, constantly being given a new face, without time having passed between one face and the next—and all these figures and faces rested, flowed, engendered one another, floated off and streamed into and through one another, and constantly stretched over all of them was something thin, an insubstantial but nonetheless existing thing like thin glass or ice, like a transparent skin, a bowl or shape or mask made of water, and this mask was smiling, and this mask was Siddhartha's smiling face, which he, Govinda, at just this moment was touching with his lips. And Govinda saw that this smiling of the mask, this smile of Oneness over all the flowing figures, this smile of simultaneousness over the thousand births and deaths, this smile of Siddhartha was precisely the same, was precisely the same still, delicate, impenetrable, perhaps kind, perhaps mocking, wise, thousandfold smile of Gautama, the Buddha, as he himself had seen it a hundred times with awe. This, Govinda knew, is how the Perfect Ones smiled.

No longer knowing whether time existed, whether this looking had lasted a second or a hundred years, no longer knowing whether there was a Siddhartha, whether a Gautama, whether a Self, an I and You, wounded in his innermost core as if by a divine arrow whose wound tastes sweet, entranced and bewildered in his innermost core, Govinda remained standing there a short while longer, bending over Siddhartha's still face that he had just kissed, that had just been the site of all shapes, all Becoming, all Being. This countenance appeared unchanged once the depths of the thousandfold immensity had closed again beneath its surface; he was silently smiling, smiling quietly and gently, very kindly perhaps, perhaps mockingly, precisely as *he* had smiled, the Sublime One.

Deeply Govinda bowed, tears of which he knew nothing coursed down his old face, and like a fire the feeling of the most ardent love, the most humble reverence was burning in his heart. Deeply he bowed, bowed to the very earth, before the one sitting there motionless, whose smile reminded him of everything he had ever loved in all his life, everything that had ever, in all his life, been dear to him and holy.

Glossary of Sanskrit Terms, Deities, Persons, Places, and Things*

Agni · Hindu fire deity, the divine personification of the fire of sacrifice.

Atharva-Veda · *see* Vedas.

Atman · The Reality that is the substrate of the individual and identical with the Absolute (Brahman); the ultimate essence of the universe; the vital breath in human beings.

banyan · East Indian tree (*Ficus benghalensis*), the branches of which send out numerous trunks that grow down to the soil so that a single tree covers a large area.

bo tree · According to Buddhist tradition, the pipal (*Ficus religiosa*) under which the Buddha sat when he attained Enlightenment.

Brahman · Impersonal spirit, the Absolute, the Eternal; the Universal essence from which all created things emanate.

---

*Many of these entries have their source in one or both of the following two works:

Luis O. Gómez, *The Land of Bliss: The Paradise of the Buddha of Measureless Light* (Honolulu: University of Hawai'i Press, 1996).

John Grimes, *A Concise Dictionary of Indian Philosophy,* 2nd ed. (Albany: State University of New York Press, 1996).

Brahmin · Member of the highest ranking social class, a class of priests.

Buddha · "One who has awakened" or "the one who has understood"; an epithet or title rather than a proper name.

Chandogya Upanishad · *see* Upanishads.

eightfold path · This path to ending desire involves: (1) right views, (2) right thoughts, (3) right speech, (4) right conduct, (5) right livelihood, (6) right effort, (7) right mindfulness, (8) right meditation.

four basic principles · The Buddha's four noble truths are: (1) All life is suffering, (2) Suffering leads to desires, (3) An end to desire brings an end to suffering, (4) The path to ending desire is eightfold.

Gundert, Wilhelm · This cousin of Hesse's was a student of Japanese religion and philology and later published a number of works on the religious history of Japan and translated the *Bi Yän Lu*, the central work of Zen Buddhism, into German.

Krishna · A widely revered and popular Indian deity, son of Vasudeva. One of his aspects is Govinda Krishna, lord of cowherds.

Lakshmi · Hindu goddess of wealth and good fortune, consort of Vishnu. In one of her incarnations, she bears the name Kamala.

Magadha · An ancient kingdom of India, situated in what is now west-central Bihar state in northeastern India. Many sites in Magadha were sacred to Buddhism.

Mara · "Lord of the Senses," a tempter bent on distracting monks and buddhas-to-be during meditation.

Maya · Principle of appearance; displays the unreal as real; brings about the illusory manifestation of the universe.

Nirvana · Liberation from passion, suffering, and rebirth; an overcoming of the wheel of birth and death (Sansara).

Om · In the Upanishads and elsewhere, a mystical word that frequently is made the object of religious meditation. Prayers and chants often begin and end with it.

pisang fruit · Plantains.

Prajapati · "Lord of Creatures," creator of the Universe.

Rig-Veda · *see* Vedas.

Rolland, Romain · Hesse greatly admired this French novelist and dramatist who, being a pacifist, donated the proceeds from his 1915 Nobel Prize to the Red Cross and later wrote a biography of Mahatma Gandhi.

Sakyamuni · "Sage of the Sakya clan," a designation for the historical Buddha Siddhartha Gautama.

sal · an East Indian timber tree (*Shorea robusta*).

Samadhi · Perfect one-pointedness of mind; absorption; the serene, unifying concentration achieved in meditation.

Samana · One of a class of wandering mendicant ascetics of ancient India.

Sama-Veda · *see* Vedas.

Sansara · The wheel of birth and death, cycle of rebirths; empirical existence.

Satyam · The real, the true; that which abides and exists beyond Maya.

Savathi · Once the capital of Kosala, the present-day province of Oudh.

Upanishads · The concluding portion of the Vedas, containing the teachings of the ancient sages; the Upanishads teach that the Self of a human being is the same as Brahman. There are ten main Upanishads, including the Chandogya.

Vedas · Sacred scriptures of the Hindu tradition, consisting of four books: Rig-Veda, Yajur-Veda, Sama-Veda, and Atharva-Veda.

Vishnu · One of the principal Hindu deities, protector and preserver of the world. Krishna is one of his incarnations.

Yoga-Veda · "Knowledge about the practices of yoga"; not one of the texts that make up the Vedas.

READING GROUP GUIDE

1. In his Introduction, Tom Robbins says that *Siddhartha* demonstrates "a hunger for spiritual illumination." What are some examples of other pieces of literature, both classic and contemporary, that share this purpose? In which ways are they similar to *Siddhartha*? How are they different?

2. Why does Siddhartha sometimes refer to himself in the third person and sometimes in the first person? What does this say about how he views himself? Consider in particular his conversation with his father on page 9.

3. The spiritual leader who came to be known as Buddha was born with the name of Siddhartha Gautama. Why does Hesse choose to give his character the same name, especially given that Hesse's Siddhartha does not decide to become one of Gautama's disciples? Similarly, why does Hesse refer to the Buddha only as Gautama, and not as Siddhartha Gautama?

4. What is the significance of Siddhartha's dream in which Govinda becomes a woman? What does it suggest about their relationship? Does it foreshadow Siddhartha's relationship with Kamala? How are Siddhartha's relationships with Govinda and Kamala different?

5. Siddhartha tells Kamala that "Perhaps people of our sort are incapable of love. The child people can love; that is their secret" (p. 63). What does he mean by "people of our sort"? Is love why Siddhartha both loathes and envies the child people? Over the course of the novel, Siddhartha explores many kinds of love—platonic, romantic, and parental. How does each affect him differently?

6. In his memoir, *Memories, Dreams, Reflections*, C. G. Jung writes that "A career, producing of children, are all maya (illusion) compared to that one thing, that your life is meaningful." For much of the novel, Siddhartha seems to embody this philosophy, sacrificing various occupations and relationships in order to seek his own spiritual purpose. But his behavior seems to change profoundly when he discovers that he has a son. Do you think that producing a child is, as Jung claims, an illusion in the face of Siddhartha's greater conquest?

7. Siddhartha looks to many people for guidance along his journey—the Brahmins, the Samanas, Gautama, Kamala, and Vasudeva. But in the end, the source that becomes most fruitful is the river. What do you think the river represents? What does Siddhartha mean when he says that his life was a river? What does Vasudeva mean when he tells Siddhartha that there are two kinds of people, one who sees the river as an obstacle and one who does not?

8. Though it is Siddhartha who sets out initially on a quest for spiritual enlightenment, several other characters—Govinda, Kamala, and Vasudeva—find their own respective fulfillment as a result of his journey. How, if at all, does this affect Siddhartha's own quest?

9. Examine the role that Govinda plays in the novel. Why is it important that he periodically revisits Siddhartha's life?

10. Siddhartha oscillates throughout the novel about his feelings toward his teachers and guides. At the end, he tells Govinda, "One can pass on knowledge but not wisdom. One can find wisdom, one can live it, one can be supported by it, one can work wonders with it, but one cannot speak it or teach it" (p. 119). Do you agree with Siddhartha? What is the difference between wisdom and knowledge?

About the Translator

SUSAN BERNOFSKY is an acclaimed translator of contemporary and modern German literature. She is a recent recipient of the Helen and Kurt Wolff Translator's Prize, a PEN Translation Fund grant, and fellowships from the American Council of Learned Societies and the National Endowment for the Humanities. Currently she is at work on a biography of the great Swiss-German modernist author Robert Walser.

A Note on the Type

The principal text of this Modern Library edition
was set in a digitized version of Janson, a typeface that
dates from about 1690 and was cut by Nicholas Kis,
a Hungarian working in Amsterdam. The original matrices have
survived and are held by the Stempel foundry in Germany.
Hermann Zapf redesigned some of the weights and sizes for
Stempel, basing his revisions on the original design.